FIREBUG

FIREBUG

Marianne Mitchell

Boyds Mills Press

To Jim, for his constant support and faith in me
—M. M.

Text copyright © 2004 by Marianne Mitchell
Cover photograph © Getty Images

Boyds Mills Press, Inc.
A Highlights Company
815 Church Street
Honesdale, Pennsylvania 18431
Printed in China

Publisher Cataloging-in-Publication Data (U.S.)

Mitchell, Marianne.
  Firebug / by Marianne Mitchell.—1st ed.
168 p. : cm.
Summary: Haley Sparks is determined to uncover who is setting fires on her
uncle's ranch.
ISBN 1-59078-170-8
1. Fires — Juvenile fiction.   2. Ranch life — Juvenile fiction.
(1. Fires — Fiction. 2. Ranch life — Fiction.) I. Title.
  [Fic] 21   PZ7.M583Fi 2004
2003108156

First edition, 2004
The text of this book is set in 13-point Minion.
Visit our Web site at www.boydsmillspress.com

10 9 8 7 6 5 4 3 2 1

147051

Juvenile
Fiction

MAR 17 2004 A

*E*VER SINCE HER MOM took the job in Seattle, nothing had gone right for Haley Sparks. Like last night, her dad had suggested spaghetti for dinner, so she offered to cook. Easy. Except she'd gotten caught up in doing a crossword puzzle and let the pasta cook for a half hour and ended up with mush-sketti instead.

And now this. Haley groaned as she pulled a handful of damp laundry from the washer tub. Her new red University of Arizona sweatshirt had somehow gotten mixed into the laundry pile. She didn't really mind that her sheets and towels were now a cool shade of pink. But Dad was going to have a cow when he saw his underwear.

She sorted through the tangle of washing, setting aside Dad's shorts and T-shirts. Maybe another cycle in bleach would make them snowy white again. Maybe he'd never notice. Maybe.

Haley stuffed the sheets and towels into the dryer and turned it on. Back into the washer went the pink underwear, along with a generous dousing of bleach. As she started the machine again, she heard the phone ring. Hoping it was her mom calling and she could get some laundry tips, she headed into the kitchen. Dad picked up the phone.

"Hi, Jake," he said. "What's up?"

Haley flipped on the small TV on the counter, keeping it on mute so she could still listen in on the conversation. Most of the time when her uncle Jake called it was because he needed a favor, like borrowing money. So far, Dad didn't look too worried about hearing from his older brother. He was telling him about Mom's new job.

"Cindi's in Seattle, at KIRO," he said, shifting into his happy voice. "No, we're not moving. She's there. We're here. Everything is fine."

Haley bristled. What a lie! Everything was NOT fine. Her mom, Cindi Sparks, was now the evening news anchor at a television station about sixteen hundred miles away. Seattle was a much bigger market than Tucson, Mom had explained when she was offered the job. More money. Good for her career.

But not good for me, Haley thought. She hated having her mother so far away. Her parents had insisted that this separation was only temporary, just to see how the new job went. Later they'd decide if the whole family should move. Haley still worried. She'd seen how separation had often led to divorce in her friends' families and she didn't want that to happen to hers.

Dad peered over his glasses at Haley. "She's right here. Want to talk to her?"

Haley reached for the phone, but then he waved her off. She sat down at the counter again and waited. Her dad turned toward the wall, mumbling a few "uh-huhs" and shaking his head. His back stiffened and Haley sensed that Uncle Jake had made his pitch.

"Can't you go to an employment agency?" he asked.

Haley wished they had a speakerphone so she could hear both sides of the conversation. Whatever Jake wanted, her dad didn't sound sold on the idea. She twisted a strand of her curly brown hair, wondering what Jake had dreamed up now.

"I don't know, Jake," said Dad. "Haley's just a kid."

Haley looked up. I am not "just a kid," she thought, quickly untangling the knot she'd made in her hair. I'm twelve—almost thirteen.

As if reading her thoughts, Dad turned to her and smiled. "Of course, she's growing up faster than I'd like to admit." He paused. "Sure, she'd feel at home at the ranch," he continued. "We've been up there often enough. Of course, not since you remodeled."

The ranch was the old homestead up in Sedona. Jake's last phone call had been to borrow money so he could fix up the main house and build some new cabins. Dad hadn't been real eager to lend him any money since Jake's other "bright ideas" had often flopped. But family is family, so in the end, he gave in.

Dad was pacing now. "Well, if it's only for a week. Actually, this might solve a problem for me, too. I've got an assignment for the newspaper up on the Navajo reservation, and I didn't want to leave her home alone." Another pause. "Yeah, I could drop her off. Just a sec."

He held out the phone. "Here. He wants to talk to you."

Her uncle's voice boomed through the phone.

"How would you like a part-time summer job, kiddo?"

"Really? Doing what?"

"I need an extra hand around here until I can hire someone permanent. This place is a guest ranch now. You'd be doing a little housekeeping, helping Alma. What do you say?"

Haley winced, thinking about today's pink underwear and yesterday's soggy spaghetti. Housekeeping was not one of her talents. Also, she'd never had any kind of job before.

"Does it pay?" she asked.

"Uh, sure, you bet," said Jake. "We'll talk about it when you get here next week. What do you say?"

Haley hated being put on the spot, especially in a phone call. She glanced over at her dad. He held out his hands signaling that it was all her decision.

"Let me talk it over with Dad. I'll call you back."

"Not interested?" asked Dad as soon as Haley hung up.

"Well, I was kind of hoping I could go along with you to the reservation. I'd like to see your interviews."

Dad shook his head. "Uh-uh. No way. It's hard enough for an Anglo reporter like me to gain the elders' confidence so they'll open up and talk. Having you around would just make it harder. Besides, this is a great chance for you to get some experience in the business world."

Haley made a face. "Cleaning cabins and washing dishes hardly counts as 'business world' experience, Dad."

"It's not like you'd be in a place you don't know or dealing with strange people. It's your uncle Jake, for crying out loud. And he needs help."

Haley felt her resolve soften. Of all her relatives, her uncle Jake was her favorite. He'd always had some special surprise waiting for her when she'd come to visit. He had a knack for knowing just what she'd been wanting. Like those turquoise cowboy boots he'd given her when she was eight. And the time he woke her in the middle of the night to watch the birth of a new colt. If he needed her help now, how could she turn him down?

2

UNCLE JAKE'S RANCH was a four-hour drive north from Tucson. By the time Haley and her dad pulled off the main highway onto Dry Creek Road, the sun glowed orange behind the mountains. Haley had hoped they would arrive while it was still light out. She always watched for that first glimpse of the red rocks peeking out from their secret canyons.

Sedona, Arizona, was famous for its sculpted red rock mountains. With a little imagination, a rock formation could be a giant thumb, a coffeepot, or a bell. There was one formation that even looked like the cartoon dog Snoopy. Haley had spent hours staring at those rocks, looking for shapes of animals or people. It was an enchanted land—a place where anything could happen.

Their car eased through a neighborhood with million-dollar homes tucked in among the pine and juniper trees. Haley tried to guess what kind of jobs these people had. How could they afford such expensive houses? They sure weren't newspaper reporters like her dad. Even her mom's new television job wasn't in the million-bucks category.

Finally, her dad turned onto the rough dirt road that wound through Coconino National Forest lands. Only a few ranches from the old days were still here, their owners refusing to let them be swallowed up by big developers or the U.S. Forest Service.

As the headlights poked through the growing darkness, Haley wondered what changes her uncle had made to the ranch. Had he finally joined the new millennium and gotten a television? She wasn't an addict like some of her friends, but there were a few shows she never missed. She didn't get her hopes up, though. Jake liked to brag that he was "just an old cowboy" with no use for TV.

Haley turned to her dad. "Do you think Jake still has his horses?"

"You bet. He's even added some so he and Rags could offer trail rides to the guests."

"How come he decided to turn the ranch into a hotel?"

"Guest ranch," Dad corrected. "Jake is counting

on people wanting to get away from it all and chill out. He set it up so the cabins are booked for a week at a time, meals and activities included. Tourism is big business up here."

He drummed his fingers on the steering wheel. "I just hope he did his homework. Building new cabins and fixing up the house cleaned out his savings. If it doesn't pan out, he'll lose everything. We'd be hit, too. I had to dip into your college fund to help him."

Haley gulped. She didn't usually worry about the family income. But she knew college cost a lot. Especially the good ones. She remembered the look her parents exchanged when she said she might want to go to law school someday. It would cost Big Bucks. But when she'd asked if she could do some babysitting, her mother had flat out rejected the idea.

"It's a lot of responsibility," Mom had said. "Plus, I don't want to put you in any situation that might turn dangerous. I've read too many news stories about wackos to feel safe about you being out there."

Haley squirmed in her seat. What would Mom think about her taking a job at Uncle Jake's place?

She probably should have called her and asked. But going to the ranch was almost like being at home. How could she object? And besides, Dad had agreed. If Mom wanted to watch over her like a hawk, then she should have stayed home. Haley shoved her worries away. For now.

When the car rumbled over a cattle guard and through a wooden gate, Haley caught a glimpse of the new sign by the entry: ROCKABYE RANCH—COME & SET A SPELL. A long driveway led up to the old stone house. Haley smiled, remembering all the times she'd come here when her grandparents were alive. It had once been a working ranch with lots of horses, cattle, and a ratty old barn. The barn was gone now, replaced by new stables.

Drawing closer, Haley thought the old house loomed larger than she remembered. Then she saw why. A wraparound porch had been added and a new shake roof put on. But still, something looked wrong. She could tell Dad sensed it, too. He muttered a quiet, "Humph!"

If Rockabye Ranch was supposed to look welcoming and homey, it really flunked. Although there were several parked cars in front of the house, the dark windows showed no signs of life. The porch light wasn't even on and no one came out to meet them.

"He was expecting us tonight, wasn't he?" Haley asked.

"Sure. I called him before we left Tucson. Maybe he's around back."

Dad parked, reached into the glove compartment and grabbed the flashlight. As soon as she was out of the car, Haley wrinkled her nose.

"Is that smoke?"

Dad sniffed the air. "Let's hope it's only from a campfire or Jake's barbecue." He waggled the flashlight at her and they tromped around to the back. The flashlight beam bounced over odd shapes in the front yard that looked to Haley like crouching bears. As she passed closer, she realized they were only lounge chairs and tables.

A small orchard of apple trees separated the house from the new cabins. An orange glow flickered through the leaves. Shouts rose in the night air, proving that someone was indeed back there. As Haley and her dad emerged from the trees, they saw the trouble.

One of the brand-new cabins was on fire.

3

*H*UNGRY FLAMES LICKED THE FRAME of the cabin's front window as smoke billowed from the roof. A boy ducked out the cabin door, coughing and dragging a suitcase. A woman shouted to him, then broke away from an older couple who'd been holding her back. She pressed his soot-streaked face to her chest, sobbing and scolding him at the same time. Rags Jacobson, the foreman, aimed a fire hose at the flames while Jake hunched over a portable pump that was sucking water from the swimming pool.

Haley's dad hissed out a cuss word. Breaking into a run, he called out, "Have you called the fire department?"

Jake shouted back, "Phone's out!"

Haley trailed after him, as if hypnotized by the flames.

Her dad pulled out his cell phone and punched

at the buttons. He scowled. "Doesn't work here!" He tossed the phone to Haley and ran to help with the fire.

Haley stood frozen in place, wanting to help but not knowing how. Her nose itched and her eyes watered from the smoke. She watched nervously as hundreds of orange sparks flew up into the inky sky, mingling with the stars overhead. What if one of those sparks started a new fire somewhere else?

After an anxious ten minutes, the smoke grew whiter as the men got the fire under control. Embers hissed as the flames sputtered out. They'd kept the whole cabin from burning, but it looked like the stuff inside would be ruined. Steam wafted through the charred windows, carrying with it the peppery smell of an old campfire.

Jake switched off the pump while her dad moved everyone away from the fire debris and over to chairs in the pool area. Alma, Jake's longtime Navajo cook, brought out blankets for anyone who was cold or wet. Rags set up a portable camp light so they could see better. A haze hovered in the air like a gray ghost.

Pulling a handkerchief from his pocket, Jake ran it across his round head. He was in his fifties, but his buzz haircut made him look a lot younger. He looked over at the people whose cabin had burned. "You two all right?" he asked.

The woman nodded. "Yes. I guess so. But my music, my guitar! All lost." She put her hand out to her son. "Zach, you crazy kid! Why did you go in there? You could have been killed."

Zach pushed a strand of wet hair out of his face. "I wanted to get our clothes and my notebooks. Sorry I missed the guitar."

Jake shook his head wearily. "I don't get it. You two had barely checked in and this happens. I'm awful sorry." He heaved a sigh. "At least no one was hurt. Meantime Miz Real, you two can stay in Cabin Two. No charge."

The woman managed a weak smile. "Thank you. But one of the main reasons for our visit here is gone. I can't go to the folk concert this weekend without my guitar. Now what'll I do?"

"Don't you worry," said Jake. "We'll get you another one."

Jake scanned the circle of guests. But when his eyes met Haley's, his tired face broke into a huge grin all the way up to his bushy eyebrows.

"Haley, my girl! That was some welcome we gave

you! I'm going to need your help now more than ever."

Haley glanced over at her dad, who was rubbing his temples, a nervous habit he did whenever he was upset. Was he worried that Jake was having another streak of bad luck?

"Hey, let me introduce you two to these fine folks," said Jake. He turned back to the woman and her son. "This here is Aquanetta Real and her son Zach from Houston, Texas. She's a famous country singer and I owe her one brand-new guitar."

Aquanetta Real switched on a brighter smile and batted her dark eyes at Haley's dad. Hugging a blanket around her shoulders and with her hair all messy, she didn't look much like a star at the moment. Zach swiped at his dirty face with the end of his T-shirt. He looked about Haley's age.

"And sitting over there," continued Jake, gesturing toward a gray-haired couple, "some old friends from Phoenix, Bill and Martha Craig."

Haley vaguely remembered them as friends of her grandparents. Mr. Craig sat with his arm draped across his wife's shoulders. His eyes were still full of fear, as if he expected the fire to start up all over again.

Sitting next to the Craigs was a girl about twenty

with silver studs in her ears and eyebrows. Haley thought she looked more like a boy than a girl with her close-shaved hair. The girl leaned toward her and said, "I'm Vivica Dove. And you are—?"

"Haley Sparks. Jake's my uncle."

Everyone mumbled hellos.

"Vivica is our granddaughter," explained Mrs. Craig, reaching over and giving her arm a pat.

Vivica leaned back in her chair and waved her arm toward the smoldering cabin. "Not a very good omen for your new place, Mr. Sparks."

"What matters is that everyone's okay," said Jake. "This is just a little bad luck to keep me humble."

"You did great, Uncle Jake," Haley said, giving her uncle a thumbs up.

"David, you can stay in Cabin Four tonight," said Jake, turning to Haley's dad. "It's not quite finished inside, so I couldn't book it. Haley, you'll be in the main house."

Haley glanced again at the burned cabin. She had a sick feeling that Jake's new adventure was off to a terrible start. She made a silent pledge to help make things go better for him.

Mr. Craig stood and helped his wife up from her chair. "We're turning in, folks. Too much excitement for these old coots." Then to Vivica, "We'll see you in the morning, dear."

"Yeah. Sure," mumbled Vivica, her attention fixed on the smoke rising from the ashes.

As Haley watched the Craigs drift back to their cabin, she thought how lucky it was that the fire hadn't been at their cabin while they were sleeping. They might not have made it out in time.

Across the yard, Rags was still poking around the ruined cabin, a fire extinguisher in his hand, dousing hot spots. Vivica wandered over and stared at the cabin, the way people do when they see a car wreck. The sturdy log walls looked okay, but black holes gaped through the roof and smoke continued to billow up.

Haley's dad stood and stuffed his hands deep in his pockets. "Could it have been an electrical problem, Jake? A short in the wiring, maybe?"

Jake shook his head. "I just had Marty Thomas check all that wiring. Bring that flashlight so we can have a look-see at the fuse box and the phone lines."

Aquanetta and Zach remained slumped in their lawn chairs by the pool. Thinking she'd better do something to cheer them up, Haley went over to them.

"Sorry about all this," she said to Ms. Real. "Let

me help you get settled in the other cabin."

Aquanetta sighed and stood up, dropping the blanket from her shoulders. "It probably reeks of smoke, too," she grumbled, reaching for her suitcase. She turned to her son, who was gathering up some of the clothes he'd salvaged. "In the morning we may have to move to a motel in town," she told him.

"No, it'll be okay, Mom. I want to stay here," said Zach, a touch of pleading in his voice.

"We'll see how it goes, Zach."

"Things will look better in the morning," assured Haley. "I hope you'll stay."

But as they headed toward Cabin Two, Haley cast a nervous glance at Dad and Uncle Jake checking out the fuse box by the house. They were both muttering and shaking their heads. Jake may have said it was only bad luck, but Haley had a feeling he was a lot more worried than he let on.

*H*ALEY'S JOB STARTED AT FIVE-THIRTY the next morning. When she entered the huge country kitchen, she was surprised to see how different it looked. Gone were the old fifties appliances her grandmother had used. A huge double-wide refrigerator sat next to a silvery eight-burner gas stove. Alma Goodluck was kneading a blob of dough for the morning rolls. She was short and round, her black hair held back in a thick ponytail. Her brown eyes peeked out from under long bangs and a smile of welcome greeted Haley when she came in.

Even though the kitchen looked new and sparkly, Alma's presence reassured her that not everything had changed. Alma had worked for her grandparents as a teenager and stayed on to help Jake. Nothing seemed to ruffle her, not even the new task of running a hotel kitchen.

Alma handed her two cartons of eggs and a bowl. "For scrambled eggs," she explained.

Haley smacked the first egg against the rim of the bowl. Yolk, white, and bits of shell all smooshed together in her hand. She carefully picked out the shells and tried again, cracking the egg gently. This time, only a few pieces of shell ended up in the bowl.

Alma sighed and cupped an egg in her hand. "Like this." Crack! It split evenly in two, dropping only the white and yolk into the bowl. Alma cracked two more, her fingers slightly spreading the shell open. "You need confidence. And rhythm."

Haley tried another egg. When it split evenly, no stray shells, she straightened her back and smiled. No one had ever shown her this technique before. By the eighteenth egg, she had rhythm, she had confidence, cracking two at a time like a pro.

When the guests arrived for breakfast, morning sunlight lit up the new porch and sparkled off the glass and silverware on the tables. Alma had set up hot pans of eggs, bacon, sausage, and cinnamon rolls on the serving table. Haley made her rounds with coffee and tea, checking everyone out.

Aquanetta posed like a movie star at her table, a cigarette dangling between her fingers. She had on a long pleated skirt, a white peasant blouse, and dangly beaded earrings. Her hair was swept back in a long braid down her back. She must like being gawked at, thought Haley. Aquanetta reminded her of Mom, the TV celebrity, always wondering how she looked.

Still wearing his grubby T-shirt and jeans from last night, Zach sat hunched over in his chair, sketching in a notebook.

As Haley poured the Craigs some coffee, a gray SUV pulled up in front. A man dressed in jeans and a plaid shirt hopped out and headed inside, nodding a brief hello as he passed.

"Must be the insurance agent," said Mr. Craig. "Hope he does right by Jake."

Aquanetta stubbed out her cigarette and got up. "I lost some valuable property in that fire and I'd like to put in a claim," her voice trailed after her as she disappeared into the main house.

Haley glanced over at Zach. He'd put down his pencil and was staring off into the mountains, his face intent, as if looking for something. She hitched up her tray and walked over to his table.

"Nice drawing," she said, noticing his sketch of a cabin.

He snapped the notebook closed. "Just doodling. What's there to do around here, anyway?"

She studied him a moment before answering. He didn't strike her as the outdoorsy type. "Well, there's hiking." She swung her arm toward the red cliffs surrounding Rockabye Ranch. "The caves around here are pretty cool."

His eyebrows went up. "Any Indian ruins in them?"

"Some, but they're not in very good shape. We also have horses. The foreman can take you on a trail ride."

"Yeah. Maybe." He went back to staring at the mountains.

Haley sighed and continued her rounds with the coffee.

Vivica sat near the Craigs, a black-and-white cat curled up on her lap, purring loudly as she rubbed his ears. He was the latest in a long line of mousers Jake tried to keep on the ranch. But domestic cats didn't last long there. Bigger cats—mountain lions, to be exact—made this area their home, too.

Vivica looked up suddenly and asked, "Anyone

want to go see the vortex over in Boynton Canyon?"

"What's a vortex?" asked Zach.

Vivica's mouth dropped open and her eyes widened. "Don't you know? Sedona is full of places where the earth's power is concentrated. If you sit in just the right spot you can actually feel the power, like energy spiraling out to the universe. It's awesome!"

"I bet," muttered Zach, not sounding too convinced.

"Lot of woo-woo talk, if you ask me," grumbled Mr. Craig.

Vivica looked daggers at the old man.

"Don't mind him, dear," soothed Mrs. Craig. "He still hasn't figured out the VCR. You go right ahead and explore."

"So, you want to come see it?" asked Vivica, turning back to Zach. "It'll be like hearing Mother Earth's heartbeat." Her eyes now glittered with excitement, and in spite of her boyish haircut, she was kind of pretty. She reminded Haley of the people she'd seen hanging around Fourth Avenue in Tucson. Retro hippie, right down to her tie-dyed shirt and sandals. Glancing out to the parking lot, Haley guessed that the old lime green VW van covered in bumper stickers was hers, too.

Zach shook his head. "No, thanks. Maybe I'll explore around here."

Vivica shrugged and went back to stroking the cat. "Suit yourself."

Haley hesitated. She wasn't sure what Jake's policy was on the help visiting with the guests. But he had told her when she wasn't working, her time was her own. Zach was the only one close to her own age, and even though he'd been a little distant to her so far, she wanted to know him better.

"You know, I used to come here a lot before my uncle made all these changes. If you want, I can show you some places to explore."

He almost smiled at her. "Sounds good. When?"

"Meet me in the living room, er, the lobby in an hour. I should be done by then."

Zach headed inside, passing Haley's dad as he came out the door. Her dad held up his hand, jangling his car keys.

"Time to go. So long, kiddo," he said, giving Haley a quick hug. "You'll be fine. But I left the number where I'll be staying in Cameron if you need to call me."

"See you in a week, Dad. Good luck with the interviews!"

When breakfast was over and the dishes cleared, Haley peeked into the living room. She still had trouble thinking of the old house in hotel terms. The only hotel-like thing in the room was the tall check-in desk with a rack of tourist brochures on one end and a basket of snacks and fresh fruit on the other.

A stone fireplace with a mounted deer head over the mantel took up most of the wall on the far end of the room. Facing the fireplace was a brown leather sofa and a low coffee table. No TV.

Zach stood near the fireplace, checking out the books in an old wooden hutch. The selection wasn't great. A few westerns, some well-worn paperbacks, local history books, and some poetry. He pulled out one of the history books and leafed through it.

"Are you into history?" Haley asked, coming up behind him.

He turned, closing the old book and putting it back on the shelf. "I've been reading up on Sedona.

It's a neat place."

"Come on. I'll show you around."

"Are you sure you can take off for this?" asked Zach.

"It's okay. Jake said one of my duties is taking care the guests. So this counts, don't you think?"

He shrugged. "I guess."

As they passed the check-in desk, Zach pointed to the clutter of postcards tacked up on the wall.

"What's with that?" he asked.

Haley paused. "Jake can explain better than I can." She called into the office, "You in there, Jake?"

He stepped out to the desk, newspaper in his hands. "Yup. What can I do for you?"

"Tell Zach about your postcards."

Jake glanced back at the wall of cards and laughed. "Oh, that. Just some silly idea I had a few years back. I was up on the Oregon coast once and I got the bright idea to put messages in a couple of bottles and see what happened. I wrote the same thing on slips of paper, sealed them in old wine bottles, and threw them out to sea."

"What was the message?" asked Zach.

"A simple one: 'Send me a postcard telling me

where you found this bottle. Then, for good luck, put the note back in the bottle and toss it out to sea again.' And I gave the address here at the ranch."

"Did it work?"

Jake waved his arm at the wall of postcards behind him. "Apparently so! The first postcard arrived about three months later from San Francisco. Made sense, a bottle floating down the coast from Oregon to California. The person wrote, 'Found your bottle under the Golden Gate Bridge. Here's your postcard. Good Luck.' But then I started getting mail from landlocked towns, like Salt Lake City, Denver, and Atlanta. Every couple of months or so, a new card would arrive. Some had the same handwriting and a similar message, so I figured the same person was doing it. Then cards started to come in from overseas with all kinds of crazy messages."

"Like what?"

Grinning, Jake turned back to the wall of postcards. He took one down with a picture of London's Buckingham Palace and read it aloud in a voice like a snooty English lady.

" 'While strolling along the Thames I found

your curious note in a bottle. Cheerio!' Signed HRH, Elizabeth Windsor."

Zach's eyes widened. "Elizabeth, as in *Queen* Elizabeth?"

"Well, yes, but not really. Now I knew someone was pulling my leg. Postcards came in from Moscow, Stockholm, Vienna, even Sydney, Australia. I asked everyone I knew but they all denied sending them."

Haley nodded. "At first he was sure my parents did it. But they swore up and down it wasn't them."

"So you never found out who sent the cards?" asked Zach.

"Nope. Haley's dad even did a story about me and my mystery cards a couple of months ago for the Phoenix paper, but no one's fessed up yet."

Haley nudged Zach's arm. "What do you think?"

Zach studied the wall of cards, then smiled. "It's easy. Anyone could post a message on the Internet and have people anywhere in the world send a card or two."

Haley shot a glance toward the ceiling. Of course! Why hadn't she thought of that?

But Jake shook his head. "Nope, nope. That may be the answer for some of the cards but not the early ones.

They go back to 1978, before e-mail and such. I just wish they'd stop coming. They're not much fun anymore."

"Not fun?" Haley asked. "What do you mean?"

Jake pinned the London postcard back on the wall. "Oh, nothin'. Never mind," he said. He picked up his newspaper again and headed back into his office.

Haley made a face. She hated when adults answered a question with "Never mind."

5

*R*ED SANDSTONE CLIFFS ROSE UP in a horseshoe formation around Rockabye Ranch. They were called red rocks but they weren't really red. Haley's dad had explained that the color came from iron ore rusting in the stone. Depending on the time of day or the weather, their colors changed. Sometimes they were salmon, pink, or violet. When Zach and Haley came out of the ranch house that morning, the rocks were showing off in deep orange.

Haley pointed past a clump of juniper trees toward the cliffs. "Let's hike up there. You'll get a great view of the whole place."

They headed through the backyard, passing Rags as he skimmed pieces of fire ash out of the remaining pool water. He was tall and lean with leathery brown skin from being outdoors so much. Haley guessed he was between twenty-five and thirty but he looked older. No matter what the occasion or weather, he always dressed the same. Black everything: hat, shirt, jeans, and cowboy boots. He'd been Jake's foreman for five or six years, but Haley didn't know much else about him.

Jake and the man from the SUV were still poking around in the ruined cabin. Someone had hauled out a pile of smoke-damaged bedding and furniture. The bitter odor of soggy ashes hung in the air.

"Too bad about your mom losing her music and guitar last night," Haley said.

"Yeah. She's been trying to make it big ever since my dad died."

"Jake said she was famous. How come I've never heard of her?"

Zach kicked at a stone. "I think your uncle was trying to make her feel good, after what happened and all. She's not really that famous. She sings in a lot of small places like bars and restaurants. She cut her first CD last year."

"My mom's in entertainment, too," said Haley, using her fingers to make quote marks in the air around the word "entertainment." "She does TV news, up in Seattle."

"I thought your family was into ranching," said Zach.

"Only on my dad's side," Haley explained. "My grandparents got this place years ago, after the old miner who owned it died."

"A miner? Like for gold and such?"

She nodded. "Kind of a hermit, too. Old Caleb Marshall never trusted anyone, especially the banks. The locals say he hid all his money here on the ranch."

Zach grinned at her. "Keep talking. This place is getting more interesting."

"Jake told me that when he was a kid he used to spend hours looking for it. He called it Caleb's Cache."

"Cash? Like in money?"

"No. A cache is something hidden."

"Did he ever find it?"

"Not that I ever heard."

Zach stopped abruptly and scanned the area. "So the old guy's treasure could still be here?"

Haley shook her head. "I doubt it. We've all looked."

"Maybe your uncle found it and kept it a secret."

"Not Jake! He would have had a celebration.

Besides, it's just a local legend. It's probably not even true."

Zach folded his arms. "Maybe I'll look around for it while I'm here."

Haley cast a wary glance back toward the ranch house. "I'm not sure Jake would want you digging holes everywhere."

"Then I'll look in places I won't have to dig up." He paused. "Want to help?"

A tingle went up Haley's spine. It was tempting. When she was little, she'd often dreamt about finding a box of money and surprising Jake with it. "I guess looking around won't hurt anything," she said.

They started up a dusty trail that took them past the newly built stables and the corral. The horses stood flicking their tails and munching hay under a tin ramada. Haley's heart quickened when she saw her favorite, a beautiful bay with a white patch down his forehead. His name was Blaze.

"Come on," she said, tugging on Zach's arm. "Let's say hello to the new horses."

Leaning on the wooden fence, Haley counted ten horses in all—Blaze, Skipper, Honey, Misty, and six new ones. She remembered what Dad had said about Uncle Jake spending all his savings on the ranch. Six extra horses would add up. Finding Caleb's Cache would sure help with his expenses.

"Do you ride?" Haley asked, turning to Zach.

"Yeah, some."

"Good. Jake's planning a trail ride for tomorrow morning."

They hiked on, skirting stubby pines and rocky outcrops. Every now and then Zach stopped her, pointing out places he thought would be good to hide something. Haley had to admit that his enthusiasm was catching. But she shook her head at each spot Zach suggested. Too many people for too many years had tried to find hidden treasure on the ranch.

The trail turned rocky and got steeper as it led to the base of the cliff. Zach paused and stared up at the shell-like cave looming above them. "Cool! Let's go there," he said, hurrying ahead. When Haley didn't follow, he called back to her, "Aren't you coming?"

"Uh-uh. Too steep," she answered. "The trail washes out partway up to that one. Besides, I'm not real fond of heights." She sat down on a nearby rock to catch her breath and shake some of Sedona's powdery red dust off her canvas shoes and socks. They'd never be white again.

Zach trotted back. "You scared?"

She glared at him. "Scared of falling down the rocks and splattering my own blood all over them. Yeah."

Zach shaded his eyes with his hand as he looked up again at the huge cave. Eons of water and wind had carved out all kinds of holes and formations in the red rocks.

"I read about caves like this," said Zach. "The Sinagua Indians might have lived up there. It would have been perfect—facing south for the sun and high enough to see if any enemies were coming." Zach sat down next to her on a rock. "You know, if I was going to hide something, that's exactly where I'd put it."

"Fine. Then you go up there. There's a rickety old ladder with only a few rungs missing last time I looked. Try it' if you want to get up to the cave. Meanwhile, I'll run back and call 9-1-1."

"You know, for someone who's supposed to be 'taking care of the guests,' you're not much fun."

Haley opened her mouth, about to fling back some snappy reply, but a flash of color through the brush caught her eye. She motioned to Zach to follow, putting a finger to her lips so he'd keep quiet. They edged around the trees and saw Vivica splayed out on her back on a wide slab of rock. She wasn't moving.

6

*H*ALEY GRABBED Zach's arm. "She's fallen!"

He leaned forward, squinting in the bright light. "Is she dead?"

Haley didn't answer. She scooted over to where Vivica lay moaning on the rock, knelt down, and touched her shoulder.

Vivica's eyes popped open and she blurted out, "Hi!"

Haley tumbled backward. "You—you scared us!"

"What happened?" asked Zach.

Vivica sat up and gaped at them. "What happened? This happened!" she said, patting the smooth sandstone slab she rested on. "The power here is absolutely amazing. I wanted to get close, to lay across the bosom of Mother Earth. Can't you feel it?"

"But you were moaning. Are you okay?" said Haley, standing up.

"Moaning? I wasn't moaning. I was humming to the harmonics of the universe," said Vivica. She grabbed Haley's hands. "Here, I'll show you. Rub your palms together."

Haley hesitated, then to keep Vivica happy, she rubbed her hands together.

"Now hold your arms out, palms down," instructed Vivica.

Haley held out her arms.

"Breathe deep."

Haley took a couple of deep breaths.

Now Vivica waved her arms like an orchestra conductor. "Open your mind and let the emotions flow out of you. Cry if you want to."

Everyone was quiet a few moments. The sun warmed Haley's back. Somewhere nearby a crow cawed and a soft breeze brushed her cheek. She inhaled the spicy scent of juniper trees.

"Do you feel the power? Do you?" Vivica asked.

Haley giggled, opened her eyes, and dropped her arms. "What I feel is silly!"

Zach slapped the sides of his jeans, dusting off the red dirt. "Weren't you supposed to be going somewhere today?" he asked.

Vivica waved him off and began collecting some

of the granite rocks scattered across the hillside. "I thought about going to Boynton Canyon, but something pulled me up here. That force," she said, jabbing her finger at the rock slab, "that force led me here. It's one powerful vortex. I'd heard that there were four of these places around Sedona. But this isn't one the books mention."

As Vivica walked around the slab, she started placing the rocks she had collected in a huge circle.

Zach stared at her, looking confused. "Now what are you doing?"

"Don't ask so many questions. Help me out here. We need to mark this place as special."

"You're really into this, aren't you?" asked Zach, rolling his eyes.

"You've just got a case of Red Rock Fever, Vivica," said Haley. "Everyone gets caught in the spell when they first arrive."

Vivica straightened up, her face aglow with perspiration. "How can you resist the spell of Mother Earth, the power of the cosmos, concentrated in these rocks?"

"This is Forest Service land up here," Haley pointed out. "You really shouldn't be moving the rocks around. It ruins the natural look of things, like carving your initials in a tree."

Vivica ignored her.

"Just trying to keep you out of trouble," said Haley with a shrug.

"Too late," said Vivica, picking up four more rocks. "My mother already kicked me out for causing trouble."

"Kicked you out? What did you do?" asked Zach.

Vivica surveyed her growing circle, then placed each rock at four points of the circle. "Let's just say we had a different idea of what I could do with my own life and my own friends."

"Is that why you're staying with your grandparents?" asked Haley.

"What's it to you?"

Haley shrugged. "Just curious. Sorry I asked." She turned and started loping back down the trail.

Zach ran after her. "Wait up!"

Haley paused and glanced back at Vivica, who was now standing in the middle of the circle, arms raised to the sky. "She says she's all for Nature but she's messing it up. What if everyone went around making rock circles?"

"But maybe she really has some special power," said Zach. "Maybe she could help us."

"Help us? With what?"

"You know, like a metal detector. Maybe she could lead us to Caleb's Cache."

Haley laughed. It surprised her how much Zach had gotten caught up in the idea of finding treasure. "I really shouldn't laugh. After all, my uncle can find water with an apple twig. He's a dowser."

"We'd have to get her to help without telling her the real reason."

"Just tell her there's another vortex around here and ask her to look for it." Haley closed her eyes again and held out her arms, palms down, letting them quiver a bit. "Ooooh, I can feel the power pulling me down into a box full of gold and money. Oooooh!"

As they galloped down the hillside, Haley saw her uncle Jake standing on the back porch, watching them. He motioned them over.

"Zach, your mother needs you," he said. "She's going in to town to look for a new guitar and wants you to come along."

"She doesn't need me for that," mumbled Zach. He stuffed his hands into his jeans pockets and plodded off toward their cabin. His shoulders drooped and Haley could almost read his thoughts: I'd rather be hunting for treasure.

Jake tapped Haley's arm and crooked his finger. "Let's go inside. We need to talk."

She followed him inside to his office, formerly known as the den. A huge wooden desk filled most of the room and cluttered bookshelves lined the walls. Heavy drapes covered the one picture window, making the room dark and gloomy. But what drew Haley's attention the most was a computer and printer sitting in the middle of Jake's desk. Maybe he was getting up to date after all!

Jake closed the door and then settled into a creaky wooden desk chair and clicked on a lamp. Haley chose a small leather ottoman facing him.

"What's up?" she asked, hoping the excursion with Zach hadn't gotten her in trouble.

Jake leaned forward and propped his fingers together. "It's about that burned cabin. I've blocked it off so no one can go looking around in there. That includes the guests—and you."

"Sure. No problem," she answered, relieved she wasn't in trouble after all. "What did the insurance guy say?"

His eyebrows twitched together, then relaxed. "Oh, the insurance. I, um, haven't called them yet. The fellow who was here earlier was one of my contractors, Marty Thomas. He was checking on wiring and such."

"Did he find out what started the fire?" Haley asked.

Jake shook his head. "No. Not yet. I'm sure it was just an accident." He leaned back in his chair and crossed his arms. "Rockabye Ranch opened for business only a few days ago, Haley, but already I've got reservations pouring in. The last couple of weeks we've been rushing like crazy to get everything ready, trying to meet my deadline. Maybe we missed a few details. I don't know. The important thing is, I want the guests to feel safe. The less talk about fires and accidents, the better, understand? If anyone asks, tell them it's all under control."

Haley got up to leave. "Yeah. Okay." At the door she paused and looked back at her uncle as he sorted through the morning mail. The way Jake dismissed the fire bothered her. Why wasn't he more eager to find out what caused it?

7

*T*HAT EVENING THE WESTERN SKY was blazing in shades of orange and yellow when Haley stepped out the kitchen door with a tray of appetizers for the guests. She shivered in her short-sleeve shirt, wishing she'd remembered her jacket. Once the daylight faded, the temperature dropped fast. Alma followed her, carrying a huge square pan of chicken pieces slathered in barbecue sauce. Together they headed for the redwood deck where the guests were gathered. Jake had built the deck over the foundation of the old miner's cabin. All that remained from the old days was a lone sycamore tree on one end and a stone chimney on the other.

Jake had seen a use for that old chimney. Using it as a flue, he had constructed his barbecue pit against the mouth of the fireplace. Sweet-scented smoke now puffed from the chimney top, as logs of apple wood turned to a glowing pile of coals inside.

Candles in red jars flickered on three tables set up on the deck. Aquanetta, wrapped in a blue flowered shawl, sat chatting with the Craigs. A portable bar had been set up and Rags was pouring a drink for Vivica. From the animated way she was talking to him, Haley figured she was trying to sell Rags on her ideas about the vortex site she'd "discovered." He looked about as excited as a dead cat.

Zach stood by the barbecue, watching as Jake fanned the coals with piece of cardboard, sending the spicy smoke into the air. Alma handed Jake the big pan of chicken.

"It's ready," she said quietly.

Jake grinned, took the pan, and slid it onto a rack in the oven. "Let the magic begin," he said, rubbing his hands together.

Alma shook her head and shuffled back to the house. Everyone always complimented Jake on his famous barbecued chicken, but Haley knew the real story; Alma did all the work while Jake took all the credit.

Haley made the rounds with the tray of appetizers. Zach zipped over to snag three stuffed mushrooms. Then he sidled up to Vivica at the bar. Haley had to force herself not to keep looking his way. The twinge of jealousy surprised her. What did she care who Zach talked to? Besides, Rags looked relieved to have another guy around.

"This barbecue brings back so many memories, Jake," said Martha Craig, waving Jake over. "It's good to be back."

He pulled out a chair and sat, giving her hand a pat. "Good to have you here, Martha. I remember how you, Bill, and my folks used to tramp all over these hills in the old days."

Bill Craig took a puff on his pipe. "Yup. Back when this was just a sleepy little town. No snooty art galleries. No posh resorts. No traffic. Just a few cabins up the creek, a couple of motels, and a general store on main street. When we came up here a couple of months ago, we hardly recognized the place."

"Our big entertainment used to be old black-and-white movies, like Ma and Pa Kettle comedies," added Mrs. Craig. "We sat on folding chairs by the horse corral right under the stars. It's sad to see all of that gone."

Mr. Craig looked up at the cliffs now glowing a deep shade of pumpkin in the sunset. "Man, I wished I'd bought land here in those days. We'd be sitting pretty. Like you here, Jake."

Jake crossed his arms and smiled.

Mr. Craig leaned forward and jabbed his pipe at Jake. "You know, I once tried to buy this place from your folks. Made them a darn good offer, but they wouldn't sell. Upped my price a couple of times and still they sat tight. You'd have thought they were sitting on a gold mine."

"I've had a few offers, too, since I made these changes," said Jake. "But I shooed them all away. I want to get Rockabye Ranch off to a good start. Then I plan to expand, put in a small golf course, maybe some tennis courts. I could give the resorts a little competition."

Mrs. Craig tut-tutted. "You can't compete with them, Jake, and you shouldn't try. This place is just right. It offers a nice escape and captures the flavor of the old days. Let's hope you don't run into any more trouble like that fire last night."

Jake and the rest of the group fell silent. Haley hustled over with the appetizers, hoping they'd talk about food instead of the fire. It didn't work.

Aquanetta speared a slice of melon wrapped in prosciutto from the tray. "We should have stayed in the first cabin you gave us, Mr. Sparks." She turned to the others and added, "When we checked in yesterday afternoon, we had Cabin One. But it was too cramped for the two of us so I asked for a larger cabin." She said to Jake, "Your insurance will cover everything, won't it?"

Jake shifted in his seat. "You bet. Absolutely."

Seeing how uneasy Jake was, Haley remembered her earlier conversation with him. The fire was the last thing he wanted people talking about.

"Um, how's that chicken doing, Jake?" Haley piped up.

Jake popped up and scooted over to the barbecue, sending her a thank-you wink as he did.

Mrs. Craig called over to him. "Speaking of the old days, whatever happened to that pal of yours from next door? You two were always climbing rocks and getting into trouble."

Jake closed the oven door, grabbed a beer from Rags, and moseyed back. "You must mean Jimmy Concannon," he said. "We lost contact some years ago. I wish I knew what happened to him."

"Hatched from the same egg, you were," added Mrs. Craig. "Never saw one without the other trailing along."

Jake chuckled and settled back in his chair. "We

spent so many hours playing cowboys and Indians and searching for lost treasure I'm surprised we ever got through school."

"And did you ever find any treasure?" asked Aquanetta, leaning forward.

Jake let a sly smile spread across his face. "One time I played a trick on Jimmy. I got all the money I'd been saving and stuffed it in an old coffee can. Then I buried it out by the barn. One day when we were out exploring, I dug it up and hollered, 'Yippee! I found it!' Jimmy came running to see what it was and I just busted up laughing."

Aquanetta's eyes narrowed. "That was kind of mean, don't you think?"

Jake shook his head. "Nah, Jimmy loved a good prank."

Laughter bubbled up from the bar as Vivica and Rags shared a joke. Zach stood awkwardly next to them, flustered, as if the joke had been at his expense.

Mrs. Craig glanced their way and shook her head. "She's been a handful, Jake."

Jake's eyebrows went up. "Vivica has?"

"Yes. When I told my daughter I'd take her in, I'd forgotten about that independent streak kids have at that age. Trouble is, she dropped out of school and has no idea how to support herself."

"We thought bringing her up here for a while might settle her down," added Mr. Craig, "give her a look at a slower lifestyle."

Mrs. Craig smiled. "I worried there might not be anything to interest her in Sedona. But maybe these vortexes she's all excited about are just the ticket."

Her husband looked over toward the bar. "Or that fellow, Rags!"

Haley followed his gaze. Vivica the hippie with Rags the cowboy? I don't think so, she thought.

8

*H*ALEY WOKE with a start. Someone, or something, was thumping against the wall. She was about to dismiss it and go back to sleep when it thumped again. In her dreams a snarly bear had been chasing her, so her first thought was that the bear was outside trying to get in. Thump! Thump! She edged the curtain back and peeked outside. Her heart jumped when a dark hulk moved across her view. Then she sighed. She recognized Blaze with his white forehead mark, munching on something right by the wall. He bumped his head with each bite. But what was the horse doing out of the corral?

The clock by her bed told her it was 3:45. She pulled on her jeans and sweatshirt and hurried outside. Jake and Rags were darting across the yard, waving their arms and trying to shoo three other horses back toward the corral.

"What happened? Why are they out?" she asked,

jogging up the hill after Jake.

"Someone let them out of their stalls," he said. He whacked his hand against his thigh, urging a black horse with wild eyes into the corral. Rags followed with Honey and Blaze.

"Where are the rest of the horses?" asked Haley, scanning the area. A nearly full moon cast a velvety blue glow over the ground. It was bright enough to see trees and rocks—and horses, if they'd been there.

"I'll saddle up and go look for them," said Rags, shaking his head in disgust. "They can't be too far off."

Jake secured the corral gate, taking an extra moment to make sure the latch locked. The area smelled of horse and manure, but Haley noticed another slight odor. Sniffing, she followed the now-familiar smoke trail to a piece of wood, smoldering by the entrance to the stables.

"Hey, Uncle Jake," she called. "Could someone have spooked the horses with this?"

Jake kicked at the blackened branch, spitting out a swear word. Bright embers still glowed in the dark. "This could have set the whole place on fire," he said. "The horses wouldn't have liked having it waved it in their faces, either."

"But who would do that? And why?" Haley asked.

Jake didn't answer, his mouth set in a tight line. As Rags rode off into the shadows, Jake stomped back down the hill to the house. Haley followed him, her head swimming with questions. First a fire and now this. Was it just another run of bad luck? Or was someone doing it on purpose?

"Are you going to call the sheriff?" she asked, trailing Jake into his office.

Her uncle spun around, his bushy eyebrows bunched together. "The sheriff? What the heck for?"

"About the horses. And the fire."

He waved her off and settled into his creaky old chair. "That fire was probably just faulty wiring. This horse business—maybe someone playing a prank. No damage from it."

"Scaring horses is no prank," insisted Haley. "Maybe someone's trying to ruin your business. You said you needed to get the ranch off to a good start. Somebody must not want that."

"That's ridiculous," Jake scoffed. "You're implying that one of my staff or one of the guests is up to no good. I can't accept that."

Haley stared at the back of Jake's computer,

wishing she could just go online and find the answers. Too bad Dad wasn't here. His reporter instincts always led him to ask the right questions. Haley would have to push for answers in her own way.

"Maybe it's someone from town who doesn't want any competition." She paused, thinking. "Is anyone mad at you, Uncle Jake?"

His face relaxed into a weak smile and he jabbed his thumb at his chest. "Mad at me? I'm just an old cowboy. I never did anybody wrong in my life. It makes no sense, no sense at all."

A question that had bugged her earlier made her ask, "What did you mean yesterday about your postcards being no fun anymore?"

He opened his desk drawer and drew out two postcards Haley hadn't seen before and handed them to her. "In the past couple of weeks I got these two. They're not in the same spirit of fun as the others."

One was a photo of some Sinaguan ruins. On the back it read, "Stop or you will be in SAD ruins, too!" The other card had a sunset on the front. The message said, "You've messed up, now your time is up! So SAD."

Haley scowled. "That's mean! And why is the

word 'sad' all in capitals?"

"Who knows?" Jake slipped the cards back into the drawer. "It's probably just some joker who heard about my crazy postcards and thought he'd be cute."

Haley leaned on his desk. "That fire wasn't cute. And those horses could have been hurt. Some are still missing."

Jake sat up and locked eyes with hers. "Rags will find them. Look, if you really think there's someone out to get me—which I doubt—I'll call David to come get you out of here. Just to be on the safe side."

Haley stared at the floor. Someone was deliberately causing trouble for Jake. Whether he believed it or not, she was committed to finding out who it was.

"No, don't call my dad. Let me help," Haley said. "I can be your extra eyes and ears. Nobody pays any attention to the hired help. Someone may say something, or do something when they think no one is around or listening."

Jake spread his big hands out on his knees and sighed. "You just go about your chores as usual. I can't stop you from being alert, but don't let your curiosity turn into spying on the guests." Turning to his computer he added, "Now if you'll excuse me, I have to figure out something to replace today's trail ride. Then I'm going to help Rags round up those horses."

Haley turned to leave.

"Wait a second," said Jake. "Here's an e-mail from you mother."

She waited while the printer rolled it out.

Haley dear,
David told me that you'd be at Jake's for the week. I wish you had talked to me about this job first. Not that you can't handle it. But you know how I feel about you being thrust out into the Big Bad World. Be good and don't give Jake any trouble. I'll call you soon to see how things are going.
Mom

Haley's shoulders slumped. Not "love Mom" or even a teeny vote of confidence. She scrunched the paper into a ball and stomped out.

9

*H*ALEY MARCHED into the kitchen and tossed the message in the trash.

Alma stood at the stove, her spatula moving sausage links around in a pan. "I heard about the horses getting out," she said, glancing Haley's way.

"Rags is finding them," Haley muttered.

"Something else wrong?"

"Nothing. Everything. Just my mother," groused Haley, throwing her arms up. "She makes me so mad!"

Alma pointed to two packages of fresh strawberries on the counter. "Those need washing and slicing."

Haley dumped the strawberries in a colander and ran them under the water. Each berry glistened like a red heart as Haley used a small knife to cut out the stems.

"Mom still thinks I'm a little girl. She's always reminding me to 'be good.' If she'd stay home, she'd see that I'm not a baby anymore."

Alma didn't respond. Haley kept coring and cutting until she had a pile of sliced strawberry hearts. She wasn't sure Alma gave a hoot about her problems with her mom but she had to talk to someone, even if it meant talking to herself.

"I mean, I'm almost grown up. I have questions for her. Girl stuff I can't talk about with Dad. But noooo, she gets a big fat offer in Seattle and she takes off. She should be with Dad and me."

A timer dinged. Alma handed the spatula to Haley.

"Watch these," she said, nodding at the pan of spitting sausages. Alma opened the oven and pulled out two pans of cornbread.

Haley's voice tensed as she poked at the sausages. "It's like she had to choose between her job and us. And she chose the job. Is that right?"

"I saw her once on TV," Alma replied, sliding the hot pans onto a cooling rack. "She's pretty."

"Yeah," Haley huffed. "Television likes it when you're young and pretty. Mom's a basket case every time she has a birthday or finds a new gray hair. She's getting old, too. She's almost forty."

Alma opened the refrigerator and took out a

chilled bowl of whipped cream. She scooped up Haley's pile of strawberries and dumped them into the bowl along with some sugar. "You're lucky," she said at last.

Haley's mouth dropped open. "Lucky?"

"Because you still have a mother. Mine couldn't take care of me. She left me at an orphanage when I was five."

"Oh." Haley stared at the floor, feeling a twinge of regret. She hadn't meant to bring up old hurts. Alma was usually so quiet, it was surprising to hear her open up about herself.

Alma put the berries and cream back in the refrigerator. "It was the right thing to do," she continued. "I had a better life there."

"Did she come see you?"

"Once. But then she got sick. She died real young."

Haley gazed out the window, remembering all the times she'd stayed up late, waiting for her mom to come home from the TV station. The late news was over at ten-thirty, which meant she didn't get home until after eleven. Haley would run to greet her, full of her own news about the day's events at school. Mom had tried to listen, but by then she was so tired, she'd hustle Haley off to bed. But at least she'd been there for her.

At least she hadn't grown up without a mother like Alma had.

A splattering and hissing from the stove made Haley jump. She'd been so caught up in her own thoughts, she'd forgotten about the sausages. Black grease sizzled in the pan as smoke began to fill the room. As Haley moved the pan off the flame, the smoke alarm went off with ear-splitting beeps. Alma hurried over to open the back door and fan out the smoke. Haley swore under her breath as Jake came charging into the kitchen.

"Problems here?" he asked.

Alma calmly shut off the alarm. "No. Just cooking. Breakfast is soon."

Jake rapped his knuckles on the door. "Good. I'm starving."

When he was gone, Haley let out a huge sigh. "Thanks," she said to Alma.

"For what?"

"For not telling him I'm a disaster in the kitchen. And for listening."

10

ABOUT NINE, a guy with spiky blonde hair arrived in a pink-canopied Jeep. Since the morning's trail ride had been canceled, Jake had arranged for the guests to go on a tour of the local sights. The Craigs and Vivica climbed aboard first. Zach hung back, not looking too happy about a touristy Jeep ride. But Aquanetta insisted that he go along, too, since she had to drive down to Phoenix for a new guitar. None of the shops in Sedona had the kind she needed.

Haley watched as the pink Jeep hurtled down the road, passing a gray SUV on its way in. She recognized it as belonging to Jake's building contractor, Marty Thomas. Maybe he had more news about the cause of the fire.

The man stepped out of his car carrying rolls of blueprints under his arm. He stopped briefly by Haley, looking worried.

"Jake in his office?" he asked.

"Yes, I think so," she said. "I saw him ride in a while ago."

Marty Thomas patted the blueprints and marched into the house, letting the screen door slam behind him.

"Now what?" said Haley to herself. She followed the contractor into the house intending to go to the kitchen. But as she passed Jake's office, she couldn't help overhearing the two men arguing inside.

"That fire was NOT caused by bad wiring," Marty was insisting. "I checked and double-checked everything myself."

"Then what caused it?" asked Jake, his voice tense.

"You tell me. You were here."

"We were all having dinner when it broke out."

"All?"

"Yes, all. What are you suggesting? That one of my guests started it?"

"No. I don't know."

A chair scraped across the floor, then creaked as someone sat. Probably Jake at his desk. Haley waited.

"Before moving out here," explained Marty, "I worked a few years with the fire department back in

Omaha. I went with our arson investigator to lots of burns. I'm no expert, but even I can tell where your fire started."

"Where?"

"On the bathroom windowsill. The whole frame is charred much more than the walls or ceiling. And something else—something I've never seen before. There's a little pile of crinkly ashes on that sill. Like burnt potato chips."

Jake harrumphed. "Potato chips?"

"Yeah. But in a way it makes sense," said Marty. "They're full of grease and they'd make a great accelerant. Once lit, they'd get things going nice and hot. Set fire to a bag of chips and, poof!"

"Only one problem with that theory," interrupted Jake. "We were all here at the house having dinner at the time. Rags came bustin' in and told me. No one had stepped out even for a minute."

"Any of your staff or guests smokers? Maybe someone left a cigarette burning. Or used it as a delay. You know, left it smoldering until it reached the accelerant."

Haley's thoughts jumped to Aquanetta. She was the only one Haley had seen smoking. But why would she burn down her own cabin?

"Or it could have been a kid, too, playing with matches," suggested Marty.

Jake's chair creaked again. "You're way off base here. I just can't see any of my guests wanting to burn a cabin. Especially those folks. They'd barely checked in. And they lost things in the fire, too."

"Then why haven't you called in the sheriff to look it over?" asked Marty.

Jake didn't answer right away. "I got my reasons."

"And they are . . . ?"

"The sheriff would ask questions. Questions about insurance."

"So?"

"I don't have any fire insurance on those cabins."

"Are you nuts?" Marty croaked. "Why not?"

"Money, of course. I'm so in debt the bank wouldn't loan me money to buy a candy bar. I spent all my savings, some of my relatives money, and even some of yours to put this deal together. There just wasn't any left over for insurance. Not yet, anyway. I was going to get it later."

"Well, it's too late for later. You just better hope that singer lady doesn't turn around and sue you."

Haley heard movement and shuffling of papers. She couldn't let Jake catch her eavesdropping. She shifted farther away from the door, ready to bolt down the hall for her bedroom if they came out.

"I want to look at that windowsill myself," said Jake. "And that mysterious pile of chips you're talking about."

The men were almost to the door when Haley ducked into her bedroom. She held her breath as footsteps thumped down the hall. From the window by her bed she watched the two men march across the yard and disappear behind the burned cabin, still arguing. A few minutes later, Marty Thomas roared off in his car and Jake headed up to the stables.

Questions buzzed in Haley's head. Marty Thomas seemed sure that someone set that fire on purpose. But why? Had her first guess been right, that someone was trying to ruin Jake's business? Could those threatening postcards Jake showed her be connected? She glanced out the window again. What she really needed was another look at the handwriting on those cards. Now was the perfect time to try.

11

As Haley eased down the hallway, she heard soft voices drifting from the kitchen. Using her fingertips, she pushed the kitchen door open a crack. Alma sat at the counter, polishing a copper pot. The voice she'd heard was coming from the radio, speaking in Navajo. The words were clipped and strange sounding until a couple of English words, like Flagstaff Chevrolet, popped out and surprised Haley with their familiarity.

She bit her lip, closing the door. The coast looked clear. Jake was up at the stables, checking on the horses. The guests would be gone for a couple of hours. In spite of the little voice in her head telling her not to be such a snoop, she edged into Jake's office. It took a moment for her eyes to adjust to the dim light. She headed straight for his desk, pausing only to glance at the geometric shapes dancing silently on the computer screen. From the center drawer she drew out the two postcards he'd shown her earlier. One postmark was so faint, she couldn't read it. On the second card, only the date was clear. It had been mailed last week.

She reread the messages, this time concentrating on the handwriting. A little scrawly, but readable. Same kind of black ink on both. They sure sounded like threats, and she wondered again why Jake wasn't more upset. I'll just borrow them for a while, thought Haley as she tucked the cards in her back pocket.

As she turned to leave, her hand brushed the computer mouse. Suddenly the screen flickered and columns of numbers appeared, replacing the screen saver shapes. Jake must have been adding up his expenses and making notes to himself. The list showed the amounts of money he'd borrowed from friends and family. She didn't know much about building costs and income, but one thing was clear. Jake couldn't afford for anything else to go wrong. If his hotel adventure failed, a lot of people, including her own parents, would lose money big time.

But now was not the time to study her uncle's finances. She needed to learn a little more about the guests, and maybe even pick up a clue. Her job helping Alma with housekeeping chores gave her the perfect excuse to go "on assignment." She didn't consider it spying as Jake had warned against. Dad had always told her that a good reporter was part writer and part bloodhound. Nose to the ground, ears alert, eyes open.

Haley went back to the kitchen and told Alma she'd take care of the cabins today. Alma agreed and showed her where the laundry cart was and explained what she needed to do.

The five new cabins, all built with smooth pine logs and tarpaper roofs, were connected by a flagstone walkway that wound past each cabin and opened onto the deck, pool, and main house. As Haley passed the pool, she noticed that all the sooty water had been drained out. Fresh water now spewed from a jet, refilling the pool. It looked so clean and inviting, Haley wished she could jump in for a swim.

She stopped her cart first in front of the burned cabin, staring at the smoke-charred window and door. Two sawhorses blocked the entrance and it still smelled like wet charcoal. She couldn't go inside, but Jake hadn't put the outside off limits. She zipped around to the back and eyed the blackened window where the fire must have started.

It didn't take a genius to see that the fire had burned hottest here. Bits of melted screening lay mixed with broken pieces of glass. And on the sill, just the way Marty Thomas had described, was a little heap of ashes, crinkled like those potato chips with ridges. How strange!

She hurried on to Zach and Aquanetta's cabin, number two. The inside had twin beds, a small bedside table, a larger writing table with two chairs by the front window, and a braided rag rug on the floor. An open closet with a rod for hanging clothes was in the back. Orange plaid curtains and bedspreads added a bit of color.

Curious how the fire spread in the other cabin, she checked the bathroom at the rear of the cabin. A fire starting on the windowsill would have set the curtains on fire. She mentally traced how the flames might have leaped from curtains to towels to woodwork and ceiling. There were no fire sprinklers in the cabin, but she noted Jake had installed a smoke alarm. The alarm's screeching was probably what alerted Rags to the trouble.

Zach had managed to save most of their belongings, judging by the stuff on the table and chairs: clothes, his mother's make-up bag, a Game Boy, and several spiral notebooks. She couldn't resist taking a closer look, but she kept her eyes on whatever was already out in the open. One spiral notebook lay open on the bedside table. The page was filled with bars of music, all done in different colored pencils. The songs looked half-finished, as if Aquanetta was trying to remember how the melodies to her lost music went. Nothing matched the ink or handwriting on Jake's postcards.

When she picked up another notebook from the floor, a folded paper fell out. It was a crude pencil map showing a house, barn, and corral. It looked eerily familiar. Jake's name was scribbled along the edge with some dates from long ago. Was this a map of how the ranch used to look? If so, how did Zach get it? She tucked the map back in the notebook, wondering if Zach knew something and hadn't told her. She'd have to find a way to ask without admitting she'd already seen it.

When that cabin was cleaned, she moved on to the Craigs'. It had the same furnishings as the other cabin but was neater. Beds were already made, clothes picked up, towels in a pile on the bathroom floor. She glanced over the clutter of brochures and papers on the desk. There were lots of real estate ads from the local newspaper and agents' cards with appointments jotted on the back.

A couple of postcards with scenes of the red rocks were propped up by the lamp. She ran her dust cloth by them, "accidentally" knocking them over. They were blank. Of course, having postcards around didn't mean anything, Haley told herself. It was a perfectly normal tourist thing.

Next to the postcards were local maps and a yellow pad full of numbers. Prices of land in 1964 in one column, today's prices in another. Wow. She could see why Mr. Craig regretted not buying land here long ago. He'd be rich now. She studied the handwriting on the yellow pad. Block letters, blue ink. Again, nothing in common with the handwriting on Jake's cards.

She skipped Cabin Four, where her dad had stayed. It could wait since it wasn't quite finished yet. Vivica's cabin, the last one to clean, was a total disaster. Bedding, towels, clothes, littered the floor. A backpack with a Love Mother Earth sticker leaned like a blob in the middle of the bed. Junk food wrappers and crystal rocks lay scattered on the table by the door. Maybe sloppy living was one of the reasons Vivica's mother had kicked her out.

Haley sighed. This was going to take an extra long time to fix up. People had no idea how hard they made it when they left their stuff all over. And she couldn't put things away for them. Or throw anything in the garbage. Alma had been very clear about those rules.

As she gathered the wet towels, she sniffed the air. Something smelled different in here. Marijuana? Or something else? Near the sink she spied an ashtray filled with ash and stubs. Little chunks of piñon incense nestled in a box next to it. Maybe Vivica burned this stuff to cover up the marijuana smell.

To strip the bed, she had to move the backpack. As she lifted it, papers, books, and crystals spilled across the floor. Sighing, she hunkered down and started collecting the papers, checking as she did for any handwritten notes to compare with the postcards.

Suddenly, a shadow darkened the floor. Haley caught her breath. Vivica leaned in the doorway, staring down at her.

12

"Am I back too soon?" Vivica asked, her head cocked sideways as she took in the scene.

Haley quickly gathered up the papers and backpack and handed them to her. "Sorry. These fell when I went to make the bed."

Vivica shrugged and blithely tossed the papers on the bed. "That's okay. You don't have to make the bed. I'll just mess it up all over again."

Haley hurried out to her cart, trying to look like the efficient maid. "How about some clean towels then?"

"Sure. But don't bother with cleaning in here."

Haley dumped a stack of towels on the table, sending a handful of crystal rocks clattering to the floor. Haley lunged for one of the crystals before it, too, tumbled off the edge.

"Oops, sorry," Haley mumbled, shifting the towels to a chair.

Vivica sighed and shook her head. "You're not really a housekeeper, are you?"

"Uh, no, I'm just helping my uncle Jake." She held the purple crystal up to the light, watching the colors dance like rainbows off the wall. "I've heard these have some kind of special power. Is that true?"

Vivica grinned. "You better believe it!"

Haley held the stone out to her. "How do they work?"

"I'll show you." Vivica pressed her hand against Haley's fingers, closing them over the crystal. "They help focus your mind and your energy. Now hold tight. Concentrate on something you really want. Let the energy flow from the crystal into your mind."

Haley squeezed the crystal and closed her eyes. Nothing. Only the warmth of Vivica's hand pressing on hers. She blinked her eyes open. "Yeah, I see what you mean," she lied, holding out the crystal again.

"Keep it. I think you could use some crystal power."

"Thanks!" said Haley, rolling the crystal between her fingers. "Where did you learn about them?"

Vivica shrugged as she leaned against the door. "I read a lot. The Internet helps. My boyfriend's the one who got me started."

"What's he like?"

"Older. Real smart. My mother hates him."

Haley blinked. "Why?"

"She's afraid he's going to steal me away."

"And is he?"

Vivica laughed. "Not exactly. If I can talk the Cs into loaning me some money . . ."

"The Cs?"

"The Craigs. My grandparents. If I can get some money out of them, my boyfriend and I are going to Mexico to see the Maya ruins at Chichén Itzá. The Mayas were really into nature, the moon and stars."

Haley stuffed the crystal in her pocket, debating whether she should ask one more nosy question. She gave in. "How come you live with your grandparents?"

"I told you. My mother did me the favor of moving me out." Vivica stepped out onto the walkway. "The Cs have been great, though. They don't spy on me and they leave me alone." She stared up at the red cliffs rising behind the ranch. "They kept saying how great Sedona was in the old days. I pictured this boring hick town full of cows or something. But I had nothing better to do, so I came along."

"They seem real disappointed with how it's changed up here."

"Yeah. But at least it's not paved over like Phoenix. The Cs are talking about moving up here. Maybe getting an old place and fixing it up."

"Really?"

Vivica reached out and put her finger to Haley's lips. "Don't say anything. It's supposed to be a secret."

"Yeah. Okay. Let me know if you need anything." Haley grabbed her cart, now piled high with dirty sheets and towels, and lumbered back to the main house, wondering why the Craigs wanted their move to Sedona kept secret.

After loading the washers with dirty laundry, Haley wandered outside again, holding her crystal up to the sun. She walked smack into Rags.

"Hey, sorry, Rags," Haley said. "Did you get the horses?"

"In the corral, safe and sound," he grumbled, shoving past her. "Some jerk cut the fences all along the east side. Not just cut, but took out whole sections. There are fresh tire tracks from whoever did it. We're lucky the horses hadn't run that far or we'd be days finding them."

Haley jogged after him, trying to match his big strides. "Can the fences be fixed?"

He stopped at a dented Chevy pickup and tossed his rope in the back. "Yeah. But I need new wire. Means a trip into town I hadn't planned on making, but I got no choice."

Inspired, Haley asked, "Can I go with you?"

Rags pulled out his keys and leaned on the open truck door. "I'm only going to the feed and hardware store."

"You can drop me at the library. It's right on your way. Then pick me up on your way back. Let me tell Alma I'm going," she yelled, sprinting back toward the house.

"Hurry up!" he shouted after her. "I got work to do."

A few moments later, Rags's truck barreled out the drive and down the bumpy dirt road, sending clouds of dust swirling. The inside of the truck looked as bad as the outside. Tools, candy wrappers, bug spray, and a few pine cones littered the floor. Tufts of padding stuck out from rips in the vinyl seat.

Rags had on his usual black jeans and black T-shirt. The only color on him was a dark blue snake tattoo crawling down his arm. It gave Haley the creeps. "How come they call you Rags?" she asked, breaking the silence between them. "You don't dress in rags."

Rags snorted as he pulled out onto the paved road. "Always hated my real name, Ragnar. Came from my Swede grandpa. Rags suits me better."

"Names are weird. I got named after the comet," she said.

He fiddled with the radio, stopping on a country music station. Songs of lost dogs, broken hearts, and lonesome highways filled the air. Rags drummed the steering wheel, then asked, "So what's in town that you're so fired up about?"

Haley shrugged. She wasn't sure what she was after. She'd picked up bits and pieces from the guests' cabins, but she felt she still needed to know more about the ranch itself. For example, was there some reason Rockabye Ranch was targeted for trouble? Since Rags could be involved, she wasn't about to let him know her plans. "I want to go to the library," she said finally.

He looked over at her like she was nuts. "On a

fine day like this?"

"I need to look up something," Haley said, staring out the window. "For one thing, I'd like to know about the old guy who used to own Jake's ranch."

"That old coot? Why in thunder do you want to waste your time on him?"

"Is it true he didn't trust banks and so he hid his money somewhere and no one has ever found it?"

Rags' eyebrows shot up. "So, that's it. You're looking to find Caleb's Cache, eh? Well, good luck, sister. Everyone and their cross-eyed grandma's been trying to find that. I've wasted too many days poking around like a durn fool. Finally gave up. Either the old man was real good at hiding things, or someone beat me to it. Or he never hid anything in the first place."

"But what if he did? Wouldn't it be cool to find it?"

He laughed. "And what would you do with it if you did? Buy out the candy store?"

Haley squirmed in her seat. "No. I'd give it to Jake. He could use the money."

Rags huffed and turned up the volume on the radio, saying, "Couldn't we all."

13

THE SEDONA PUBLIC LIBRARY was a low L-shaped building built with walls of red sandstone that reminded Haley of stacks of books. A statue of the town's namesake, Sedona Schnebly, stood in front holding out a basket of apples. She and her family settled in the area in 1902. Haley thought it must have been even more beautiful back then without all the hotels, shops, stoplights, and highways everywhere.

Haley started her search at the computer terminal, typing in "Sedona." A raft of titles came up, most located in the nonfiction area. She wandered over to the 900 section, hoping some title would jump out at her. After pulling out books on rock climbing, vortex sites, and tourist guides, a better idea hit her.

Last year in school when she'd done a report on

Bolivia, she'd learned that the reference librarian was the one to go to for information. "They live to answer questions," her teacher had said. So Haley headed to the reference desk where a name plate read "Miss Little." The name suited the woman sitting there. She was skinny with a small face framed by tightly permed gray curls. She looked up when Haley stopped at her desk.

Haley explained what she was searching for.

Miss Little pushed her glasses up on her nose a bit and looked her over. "Old Marshall place? There was some talk about that property a little while ago. Follow me." She strode over to a long row of wooden files and opened a drawer. Pulling out a small box she chuckled. "Oh, my age is fooling me. That was over forty years ago!"

Haley followed the librarian to a microfilm viewer and watched as she threaded the film from the box. A blur of black-and-white pages whizzed by until suddenly Miss Little stopped, read, and scrolled down. "Here it is." She pressed a button and printed out a copy of the newspaper article. The print was tiny and hard to read but Haley scanned the article anyway.

MARSHALL RANCH SOLD FOR $10,000

Local rancher Joseph Sparks is the new owner of the Marshall Ranch, located ten miles west of town, off Boynton Pass Road. The property had been tied up in the courts ever since the death of Caleb Marshall last spring. It sold for $10,000, the amount of unpaid property taxes.

The Yavapai County Sheriff Department has had its hands full keeping looters off the ranch. Marshall, a retired miner, was rumored to have buried his savings somewhere on the land. The new owner, Joseph Sparks, says he plans to graze cattle, not hunt for treasure.

"Joseph Sparks was my grandfather," explained Haley.

Miss Little sighed. "My brother and I used to go hiking in the hills around there. It's some kind of bed-and-breakfast now, right?"

"Yes. My uncle calls it Rockabye Ranch."

Miss Little smiled. "Fine name for a quiet out-of-the-way place."

Haley's fingers closed around the crystal in her pocket, willing her brain to focus. "Is there any other information about the history of that ranch, or about my uncle, Jake Sparks?"

"Let me see," said Miss Little.

She went back to her desk and checked her computer. Then she led Haley over to a row of huge drawers. She pulled out one marked "local history" and handed over a folder full of news clippings.

"These haven't been microfilmed yet. Handle them carefully. They're getting ragged."

Miss Little turned to help another library patron. Haley stood at the drawer, gently unfolding and reading old clippings. Three articles were about Sedona's 100th birthday celebration and people who had been part of the town's history, including her grandfather, Joseph Sparks. Several articles touted the pros and cons of the vortex craze. In 1987, five thousand New Agers came from all over for something they called a Harmonics Convergence. They formed circles at vortex sites and chanted, some hoping to be lifted from Earth and carried off to the galaxy of Andromeda. Vivica would have loved that, thought Haley. Attached to the article was a simplified tourist-type map showing where all the main vortex sites were in

Sedona, including the one at Boynton Canyon that Vivica had mentioned. The ranch itself wasn't marked, but the cliffs behind it were, including the boundaries of the Forest Service land.

Haley was about to put the folder back in the drawer when her eyes locked onto a small obituary column. The name Concannon jumped out at her. It said that former Sedona resident James Concannon had died in a rodeo accident, leaving behind his wife, Marisol, and a ten-year-old son, Zachary. Jimmy was Jake's childhood pal, Haley remembered. He'd probably like to know what had happened to his friend.

She glanced up and saw Rags standing awkwardly in the entrance. He pointed at her and then jabbed his thumb toward his truck, waiting just outside. He looked antsy to leave. She put the materials and folder into the drawer and went back to Miss Little's desk.

"Thanks for your help. I have to go now. Rags is here and he's my ride back to the ranch."

Miss Little peered over her glasses toward the door. Her eyes narrowed and she muttered, "I'm surprised your uncle would have Rags Jacobson around his place, now that it's a hotel and all."

Her comment startled Haley. "Why?"

"Trouble seems to follow that boy. He even spent a while in jail."

Haley's mouth went suddenly dry. "He did? What for?"

Miss Little turned to her computer, shaking her head. "Perhaps your uncle can fill you in."

"Thanks," Haley whispered. She grabbed her bag and headed for the door, wondering what Rags could have done that had landed him in jail.

14

THE NEXT MORNING, Haley sat on the wood fence railing around the corral watching Jake and Rags assign horses to Aquanetta, Zach, and Vivica. The Craigs had begged off, claiming creaky knees and stiff joints. But Haley knew from her job as the observant maid that they had an appointment with a real estate agent that morning.

Aquanetta, wearing well-worn boots and riding pants, was helping Vivica and Zach pick out riding helmets. Haley counted six horses, saddled and ready. Three for guests. One each for Rags and Jake, and one for . . .

Jake shouted over to Haley, "Come on. You want to go, don't you?"

Grinning, Haley jumped off the fence, grabbed a helmet from the rack, and joined the group. She had her eyes on the big brown horse, Blaze. He was the oldest in Jake's stable, but Haley liked him best and always asked to ride him.

Jake turned to Aquanetta and asked, "How much riding experience have you had?"

"Quite a bit," she replied confidently. Jake nodded to Rags who brought a palomino gelding over to her.

"This is Skipper," said Rags. "He's a frisky one, but he'll listen to you."

Aquanetta swung herself easily into the saddle and Rags adjusted the stirrups for her long legs.

"Zach, how about you? Ridden much?" asked Jake.

"Some. Enough not to fall off," Zach said.

Jake brought over a dappled-gray horse. "Misty will be good for you. Not too jumpy, not pokey, either."

When Zach was settled, it was Vivica's turn. She looked a little pale.

"They don't bite, do they?" she asked, shrinking back and eyeing the horses.

"No," said Jake with a reassuring smile. "They all promised not to eat the guests. I take it you haven't ridden much?"

She gave her head a quick shake. "Not ever."

Jake nodded, glancing briefly at Haley. "Then I'll

give you Blaze. He's real gentle, though he likes to stop and graze a lot. Nudge him a little with your knees to keep him moving."

Haley's heart sank as she watched Jake hand over her favorite horse to Vivica. It took three tries with Jake's help before Vivica was mounted. Old Blaze just stood there, eyes half-closed, not minding a bit that he had to have a greenhorn on his back.

As if reading her thoughts, Jake said to Haley, "I know. He's your pal. But I have a new horse for you, and I'm sure you'll get along just fine."

Rags led a muscular black horse with huge dark eyes to her. "This is Ringo," he said, handing her the reins.

Haley ran her hand across his warm velvety cheek. His ears twitched and he bobbed his head, as if saying hello. "Good boy," said Haley. She stepped into the stirrup and pulled herself up. On the first try. She smiled grandly at Vivica.

Vivica didn't smile back. She sat stiff in the saddle, looking scared to death.

Jake passed out water bottles to everyone. "You forget how dry it is up here. No water fountains on the trail, either."

Haley tucked her bottle into a little saddlebag.

Alma handed up a knapsack to Jake. Haley hoped it was those fresh-baked cookies and thermoses of coffee she'd seen in the kitchen.

When they were all up and ready to go, Jake led the way out of the yard. Aquanetta, Haley, Vivica, and Zach followed. Rags brought up the rear, to make sure no one fell behind or got lost.

The trail soon left the wide open spaces of the ranch and began a slow but steady climb up the rocky hillsides. Haley stared at the wall of red sandstone cliffs on her left that blocked the morning sun. To her right, the ground sloped downward to fields of pine, juniper, and the occasional prickly pear cactus. Above her, puffy white clouds floated in a sea of powder blue. The cool air up here was clear and sharp, not hazy and dusty like it was sometimes in Tucson. Haley took a deep breath of piney air. It smelled like Christmas.

Ahead of her, Aquanetta sat serenely on her horse, swaying smoothly with his gait. Haley tried to will her own body to stop bouncing up and down as she rode. Her legs would hurt tonight for sure. She reached forward and gave Ringo's silky neck a pat.

The group rode on in silence and Haley let her mind go blank, shutting out for a while all the questions that had been bothering her. Instead, she concentrated on quiet sounds of the trail. A soft breeze whispered in the pines. Dozens of birds mixed their morning songs with the rhythmic clop-clop-clop of the horses' hooves. She gazed across the valley below, where the land was still rough and undeveloped. No houses, no malls, no galleries. It probably hadn't changed much since Sedona Schnebly arrived here a hundred years ago.

Suddenly, cross words shattered her reverie.

"Dumb old horse!" snapped Vivica from behind her.

Haley turned in her saddle to see what the problem was. Blaze had stopped dead in his tracks and was munching on a clump of grass.

Vivica jerked the reins. "Come on!" she urged, giving his sides a hard kick. Blaze threw back his head, whinnied in protest, and bolted forward, bumping into and startling Haley's horse.

Ringo jumped off the trail and galloped into the brush. He lunged past boulders the size of small cars, Haley's heart thudding with every hoofbeat. She tried slowing him by pulling back on the reins but he wasn't responding. A scraggly pine branch whipped against her arm, making her drop the reins. Desperate not to fall off, she grabbed the saddle horn with one hand and a chunk of Ringo's mane with the other. Suddenly, another horse and rider loomed beside her in a blur. Ringo must have thought it was a race. He sped up.

Haley screamed, "No!"

From the corner of her eye, Haley saw a slender arm reach out and grab the trailing reins. "Whoa, whoa boy," called Aquanetta, slowing her horse and Ringo at the same time. Finally, Ringo shuddered to a stop as red dust swirled around them. He snorted, sending a shiver through his whole body. Haley let out a sigh of relief, though her heart kept on pounding. Tears welled in her eyes.

"Are you all right, honey?" Aquanetta asked, handing the reins back.

Haley's mouth twitched a smile as she blinked back her tears. "Yes. A little scared, but okay. Thanks!"

Aquanetta brushed the dust off her riding pants and grinned over at her. "You did a good job of staying on. That horse was really moving."

Jake and Rags came skittering down the slope. "What happened there, girl?" asked Jake, pulling up beside her.

"I don't know," Haley answered, her mouth dry and dusty. "Blaze bumped into us."

Rags sat shaking his head.

Haley stared at him. "What? I didn't do anything."

"Not saying you did," he mumbled. "Just think we have our hands full keeping the guests safe. You're gonna ride with us, you gotta stay in control."

Haley's mouth dropped open. It wasn't her fault. Rags should be scolding Vivica, not her!

Jake turned his attention to Aquanetta. "You sure reacted fast, Miz Real. Ever do competition riding?"

Aquanetta smoothed a strand of hair out of her face. She fell silent a moment, her dark eyes far away. "A little," she replied softly. "Some rodeo. Some barrel racing."

Jake's hand touched the brim of his hat. "My compliments, ma'am. And my thanks for rescuing my niece."

Haley pulled out her water bottle and took a long drink. She stared up the hillside to where Vivica sat calmly on Blaze, who was once again munching the greenery. For a moment, Haley wondered if Vivica had made him bolt on purpose. Would she have done that? Now Haley wished she hadn't sent Vivica that smug little smile when they started.

The group re-formed in a line on the trail and continued plodding along. This time Zach stayed behind Haley and Vivica rode in front of Rags. Haley hoped he'd keep an eye on her and make sure she treated Blaze right so something else crazy didn't happen. As the trail wound into a canyon with steep drop-offs at the edge, Haley glanced nervously at the valley below. Ringo better not get spooked again.

15

*T*O HALEY'S RELIEF, the rest of the ride finished with no more runaway horses or other troubles. Vivica was all smiles when they got back into the yard, even though she winced when she got off Blaze. Haley sympathized, knowing her own legs would also ache by the end of the day.

Ringo and Misty stood tied to a hitching post outside the stables, waiting for their brushing down after the dusty trail ride.

"Let me take your saddle in," said Zach.

Haley undid the cinch and pulled off the heavy saddle. She handed it and the blanket to Zach. Even though the trouble on the trail hadn't been her fault, she'd offered to help Rags put the horses away afterward. She was glad Zach had joined her.

Zach returned with a bucket of brushes. Haley grabbed a curry brush and began stroking Ringo's neck and shoulders. The big black horse smelled of sweat and dust.

As Haley brushed and curried Ringo, she watched how Zach moved around the horses, patting them as they shifted and snorted. He seemed perfectly at ease with them. Did he have more horse experience than he let on? Other bits of information were bugging her, too. Was it just a coincidence that Jake's boyhood pal, Jimmy Concannon, was a rodeo rider with a son named Zachary? And what about Zach's mom admitting to doing some competition riding? These doubts itched at Haley like mosquito bites begging to be scratched.

Zach lifted Misty's rear hoof and began cleaning dirt and debris out with a pick. Now how would a city boy have known how to use a hoof pick?

"You're very good at that," Haley commented.

He didn't look up but kept cleaning the hoof. "My dad taught me."

"Before he died?"

"Yeah." Zach finished with one hoof and started on another one. "So where'd you learn to curry?" he asked, dodging Misty's tail as it flicked at the buzzing flies.

"Right here," said Haley. "Jake showed me how last summer when I came up with my parents. He didn't have so many horses then. He could sure use some help now."

They finished the grooming in silence and then led the two horses out to the corral. After taking the halters off, Haley fished a couple of sugar cubes from her pocket and gave Misty and Ringo a reward. Sensing there were goodies to be had, Blaze trotted over for his share. He nudged his big brown face into Haley's chest, blowing his warm breath on her.

"You do remember me, don't you, big guy?" said Haley.

Zach patted Blaze's neck. "Wish my mom and I could stay up here. I like working with horses."

"Doesn't your mom have a job to go back to?"

He shook his head, frowning. "No. Not lately. She's been looking for a permanent gig. But so far, she's only had temporary jobs. Since my dad died, we move a lot. In the past five years I've been at six different schools."

Haley made a face. "Ugh. I'd hate that." As much as she resented her mom taking a job in Seattle, she was glad the family didn't have to move. At least not yet. She mentally chalked up one point for Mom for not yanking her around like Zach's mom had done.

Her thoughts brought her back to questions about Zach's dad. Who was he? How did he die? She was still curious about the obituary she'd seen at the library.

"Did you ever live here in Sedona?" asked Haley, trying to work the conversation back to his dad.

"Uh-uh. This is my first time here. Why?"

Blaze nudged Haley's arm looking for more sweets. She gave him a hard pat and sent him away. "I was at the library yesterday trying to find out some history about the ranch, maybe even something about Caleb's Cache. Anyway, I came across a story about my uncle's friend, Jimmy Concannon. It was an obituary."

"So?"

"So, it said he was killed in a rodeo accident. And that he was 'survived by his wife, Marisol, also a rodeo rider, and a ten-year-old son, Zachary.'"

Zach didn't reply. He kept his eyes on Blaze as the horse trotted back to the ramada to join the others.

"Your mom rides like a pro. She said she'd ridden in rodeos, too. Maybe even met a guy named Jimmy there?"

Zach leaned against the corral fence, his arms crossed, and gave Haley a hard look. "So, what's your point?"

"I was just wondering . . . you were ten about that time. Your name is Zachary. Was that article about your dad?"

Zach turned back to the horses. "My mom's name is Aquanetta."

"A stage name, I bet," said Haley. "Nobody's really named after a hair spray."

"You sure ask a lot of personal questions, you know?"

Haley laughed. "I know. I get it from my parents. They're both reporters. Asking questions is kind of a family habit." She fiddled with the halters in her hand, getting up the nerve to ask him a really direct question. "So, was Jimmy Concannon your dad?"

He shrugged. "What of it?"

Haley felt a rush of victory. "Then why the big secret? Why not tell Jake? He'd be psyched to know who you are."

Zach waved his arm toward the cabins. "I wanted to scope out the place first. My mom had to come up here anyway for the concert, so I talked her into staying here. We'd heard how Jake had fixed up the ranch, and we wondered if he'd come into a wad of money."

"Hardly! Jake used his savings to redo this place. He even borrowed money from my parents. Besides, what business is it of yours where he got the money?"

Zach lowered his eyes and sighed. "It's about Caleb's Cache."

Haley stared at him open-mouthed. "You knew about that all along?"

"Some of it. I wanted to know if Jake had found it and gypped my dad out of his share."

"*His* share?"

"It's a long story."

Haley put her hands on her hips. "I love stories. Start talking."

Zach turned and looked up toward the cave in the cliff behind them. "One time, when my dad and Jake were kids, they climbed up to that Indian cave. They sat up there eating sandwiches they'd brought along for breakfast. They'd been looking for arrowheads and stuff. But when they started to go back to the ranch, the path down was blocked by a mountain lion. They were so scared that cougar was going to have them for breakfast."

"But they got away, obviously," said Haley, impatient to hear the end.

"My dad still had a half sandwich left, so he tossed it toward the cougar, but off into the trees. When the cougar ran after it, he and Jake escaped. Jake swore that trick saved his life and if he ever found Caleb's Cache, he'd split it with my dad, fifty-fifty. My dad always believed it was still here and that it would be worth a fortune if anyone found it."

"But no one has," Haley reminded him.

"How do you know?"

"Because Jake told me, that's how."

"He could be lying."

Haley squinted at him. "Are you calling my uncle a double-crossing rat AND a liar?"

Zach shook his head. "Naw. He's nice, your uncle. He doesn't seem the type to go back on a promise. And besides, I don't think he even knew about Mom and me. Don't tell him yet, okay?"

Haley shrugged. "So the plan was, you were going to come up here to Rockabye Ranch and try to find Caleb's Cache."

"Or get Jake to admit he'd found it."

"So that's why you were so interested in exploring. I thought you were just looking to kill time."

He flashed her a look full of mischief. "You have to admit, it's neat to think there might be treasure here just waiting for us."

Haley gave him a long hard stare. "It was your cabin that caught fire. Was that part of your plan, too?"

"No way!" he snapped. "We lost a lot of stuff, remember? We don't want to torch the place—just see if we have a share in it."

Haley paused a moment, remembering what Marty Thomas had suggested. "Maybe your mom got careless, left a cigarette where it smoldered . . . "

"I doubt it. She's pretty careful. Besides, fire investigators can tell about stuff like that."

Haley thought about the potato chip ashes but decided she'd better not say anything. She wasn't supposed to know about them.

Zach was looking at her kind of funny. "Are you saying the cabin fire wasn't an accident?"

Haley scuffed her boot in the dirt, tracing a line with the toe. Jake had warned her against talking about the fire to the guests. Plus, she still wasn't convinced that Zach or his mom had nothing to do with it.

"I don't know what caused the fire," she said, not meeting his eyes. "I'm just curious about it, like anybody else."

As they headed back into the stables, an awkward silence hung in the air. Zach's confession meant that he—maybe his mom, too—had come here for a specific reason. Money. Even if their motive was silly, like looking for a treasure that may not exist, it still made Haley suspicious. How far would they go to get money from Jake?

Haley hung up the halters by the tack room door. "Look," she said at last, "I have to help Alma get dinner ready. You go right ahead with your treasure hunt. I don't think you'll find anything, though."

Zach let a sly smile tug at his cheeks. "Don't be so sure!"

16

*T*HAT NIGHT, snug under her covers and with Jake's cat curled at her feet, Haley tried to sort out all the clues she had gathered. Who would want to sabotage Rockabye Ranch? Who would hate Uncle Jake so much?

Mr. Craig said he'd once offered to buy this place from her grandparents. Was he still mad they turned him down? And why was it such a big secret that they were looking at property in Sedona? If Jake's business failed, would they try to buy it cheap?

What about Zach and his mom? They were at Rockabye Ranch because they thought Jake had cheated his old friend, Jimmy. And did those postcards have anything to do with what had been going on?

With a jolt, Haley remembered she still had the cards she'd taken from Jake's desk. She had to put them back before he noticed they were missing. She shooed the cat off the bed, got up, and padded down the dark hall. Jake's office was inky black, the heavy curtains keeping even the tiniest ray of moonlight out. She reached for the light switch but stopped. No, somebody might see it and then she'd have to explain what she was doing there. A rustling sound made her catch her breath. Had that darn cat followed her in? Or was someone else in the room? A chill ran over her skin. A faint scent floated in the air, something she'd smelled before but couldn't place.

Haley heard a scuffling as someone lunged by her, knocking her off balance. She fell backward, tumbling over the ottoman and onto the floor. Shaking, she crawled toward the pale light of the hall just as the lobby door closed and a shadowy figure slipped out into the night.

Haley scrambled to her feet and dashed outside, searching the yard for some sign of movement. A full moon bathed the trees, cars, and cabins in a silver glow. But nothing moved. No horses. No people. Not even a cricket chirping the brush. Who had knocked her over, and how had they gotten away so fast?

Defeated, Haley threw her arms up and gazed

into the sky. A zillion stars blinked down at her, making her feel small and helpless. If only she could have grabbed an arm or a leg, she would have known who'd been messing around in Jake's office. Maybe even who'd caused the fire.

She walked back inside and plopped down on the sofa. If that rotten sneak came back, she was going to be ready. Night noises slowly came back, one by one. Crickets restarted their chirping. The old house creaked as the night cooled. Haley could even hear Jake's rhythmic snoring from down the hall. Her eyelids drooped and she slipped into a fitful sleep.

In her dreams, the ranch house was crawling with people. Jake moved in and out of view and so did Zach. But other people were strangers. Bright lights made her eyes squint and her mother's face suddenly loomed in front of her. A microphone followed. "So, young lady, what do you have to say for yourself, causing all this trouble?"

"What did I do?" Haley cried, backing away.

"Do? My dear, you've ruined everything," said her mother, closing in. "The horses have all flown off, the cabins are burnt to a crisp. How many times have I told you not to leave the stove on?"

"But I didn't do it, I swear!"

Her mother backed away and looked straight ahead into the camera.

"This is Cindi Sparks reporting live from Seattle. A poor girl, starving for attention, has pointed an accusing finger at . . ."

The camera panned the room. Haley strained to see who her mother was talking about, but the faces were all a blur. Someone was poking her and calling her name, but she kept pushing them away. She woke up to find her uncle leaning over her, tapping her shoulder.

"What? What's wrong?" she sputtered, surprised to find herself stretched out on the sofa in the living room. Daylight streamed in the window.

"I was about to ask you the same question," Jake replied. "Why are you sleeping out here?"

Haley rubbed her eyes, trying to shake off the dream. She ran her hand through her messy hair, groaning as she realized that it was probably sticking straight up. "Someone was out here last night. I stayed to see if they came back."

"Did you see who it was?"

"No, it was too dark."

"Well, someone was here, all right." He paused

and narrowed his eyes at her. "Did you happen to use my computer last night? You know, send an e-mail to a friend or play a few games?"

Haley pushed herself up, miffed. "No way. I know better than to use someone else's computer without asking. Why?"

"Come look." Jake led the way down the hall to his office. "My computer's got a virus. All my records, all my accounts, reservations for the next six months, orders for the business, credit card info, everything is gone."

Haley gaped at the screen. A demented-looking Smokey Bear leered back at her then disappeared in a puff of smoke, only to reappear and glare at her again. Over and over—bear, smoke, bear.

"Don't you have an antivirus program?" Haley asked.

"Sure I do. The best there is," Jake said, patting his monitor. "But somehow, it got turned off. That left the barn door open for any old fox to slip in."

"Or bear," mused Haley. She thought about that for a moment. "Could your antivirus program have been shut off by accident?"

He shook his head. "Nope. Shutting off the program takes deliberate steps. Not something

I could do by hitting the wrong key."

"Then it must have been that creep I saw sneaking around last night."

Jake sighed. "Probably so. Someone sure wants to complicate my life."

She tugged at her long T-shirt, wishing she'd gotten dressed before leaving her room last night. "But why?"

"Beats me." Jake turned back to his keyboard and punched keys, but nothing changed on the screen. He picked up two postcards and held them out to Haley. "Found these on the floor, too. They're supposed to be in my desk drawer."

Haley gulped. She was about to confess that she'd borrowed them when he held out a third card.

"And this was left by the computer."

It was a new postcard. The Chapel of the Holy Cross, right there in Sedona. She took it and turned it over. No stamp and no postmark. The message read, "Say your prayers, mister." Like a signature, the initials S.A.D. were printed at the bottom. Who was S.A.D.? She quickly ran down the names of everyone at the ranch, guests included. No one had those initials. Was an outsider causing this trouble after all?

One thing was certain. Someone wanted Uncle

Jake and Rockabye Ranch to be ruined. First the fire, then the horses set loose and the fences cut. Now a virus in the computer. How would Jake run his business? Who would benefit if he went broke?

*L*ATER THAT MORNING, Haley stepped out of the laundry room, a stack of clean towels in her arms. A warm sun shone down from a bright blue sky promising a perfect day for doing nothing. Haley sighed. Although Alma was cleaning the cabins today, Haley still had her share of chores. She peered over the towels as she passed by the pool, wishing she could just goof off.

Soft guitar music drew Haley's attention. Aquanetta sat perched on a chair, strumming on her new guitar. After playing a few chords, she'd jot them down in her music book. Resting in a tray full of ashes, a lit cigarette sent a tiny plume of smoke Haley's way, making her nose itch. She wondered why a singer would risk hurting her voice by smoking.

In the pool, Vivica was swimming laps, cutting through the sparkling water like a dolphin. Nearby, Zach sat hunched over on a chair, studying a tattered piece of paper. He looked up, caught Haley's eye and waved her over.

"What's up?" she asked, hugging the stack of towels.

He held out the paper. "I wanted to show you this. It was my dad's."

Haley turned her head and looked at it, recognizing the map she'd seen in his cabin. Pretending surprise, she asked, "What is it?"

"It's a map of this place, in the old days, before all the changes."

"Cool," said Haley. She put down her load of towels on a table and looked closer at the map. "No cabins, no swimming pool. There's Grandpa's ratty old barn." Small marks on the map caught her attention. "What are those?"

"Those are places Jake and my dad looked for the old guy's stuff."

Aquanetta's hand thumped against the guitar, stopping the music. "Would you two take your treasure hunt someplace else?" she grumbled. "I'm trying to work here."

"Sorry," said Haley, picking up her towels again. As she headed toward the cabins, Zach followed.

"She still hasn't told Jake who she is?" Haley

asked, glancing back at Aquanetta.

"No. Not yet. But she will. All she can think about now is the concert on Saturday. So, do you want to go?"

"To the concert?"

Zach gave the map a shake. "No. I meant go look for the cache."

"There is no cache, silly. It's just a story."

"How can you be so sure? This at least tells us where *not* to look."

Haley glanced at the map in his hand. She didn't want to waste her time hunting for worthless junk or moldy old papers. But what if they found something really valuable?

"First I have to help Alma for a while," said Haley. "Then I can meet you—there." Haley pointed to a small circle on the map. "What's that?"

Zach looked where she was pointing. "I think it's a well. But I haven't seen any well around here." He nodded up toward the horses. "Looks like that circle should be where the stables are now. You know, a well would be a great place to hide something."

"Don't you think someone would have checked that out already?"

Zach folded the map and tucked it under his

arm. "Not if the well is covered up or hidden."

"Okay. Anything beats doing dishes or sweeping cabins. Meet me at the stables in an hour."

Before going to meet Zach, Haley brought Jake a mug of coffee and a couple of rolls. She thought he needed cheering up.

"I'll never figure this out," he muttered, taking a sip of coffee.

"You look unhappy," said Mrs. Craig, sticking her head in the office.

Jake looked up. "That's for darn sure. My computer got a virus last night. All my files are gone and I haven't a clue how to get them back. Or even if I can."

"Jake lost all his billing information, reservations, everything," Haley added.

Mrs. Craig came over to the computer. "Move over, young man," she ordered, nudging Jake out of his chair. "I think I can help you out here."

Jake stared at her, his eyes wide. "You know something about retrieving lost files?"

Mrs. Craig sat down and started tapping on the keyboard. "I was a school librarian for thirty years and when computers came on the scene, they put me in charge of the computer lab. What I didn't learn from the manuals, I learned from the kids. When I retired, I got a part-time job with a data retrieval company." She looked up at Haley and winked. "We golden oldies gotta keep up, you know."

Jake chuckled. "Well, if that don't beat all! I guess if she can find my lost files, that'd make her a golden retriever!"

Mrs. Craig laughed and got to work. "This may take a while, but I'll do my best."

Haley edged out of the office, leaving the two to sort things out. But a small doubt nagged at her. If Mrs. Craig knew so much about computers, she'd also know how to send someone a virus. And she'd come out looking good by offering to help fix the damage. Haley shook her head. Everyone was looking suspicious to her now. She had to focus. She fumbled in her pocket and squeezed Vivica's crystal, wishing it would help.

Outside in the apple orchard, Haley's eyes wandered from tree to tree. If she was going to help Zach look for that old well, she needed a fruit branch. It had to be just the right shape. Not dried out or too thin, but fresh and strong. Finally, she spied a Y-shaped branch, perfect for her needs.

"Thank you, tree!" she whispered as she began sawing it off.

"Do you often talk to trees?" said a voice behind her.

Haley swung around and smiled at Vivica.

"It's for an experiment. Want to help?" asked Haley.

"Maybe. What are you trying to do?"

Haley hesitated as she put down the handsaw. To anyone else, her idea would sound too stupid. But knowing Vivica's interest in the Power of Nature, it was a good bet she wouldn't even flinch.

"I want to locate an old well. My uncle uses dowsing rods or fruit branches when he's out looking for water sources. I thought I'd try."

"You've done this before?"

Haley shook her head. "I've only watched my uncle do it." She swished her forked apple branch in the air. "Come along if you like. I know a good place to try this out."

They headed up the hill to the stables. Zach stood outside the wide doors with a quizzical look on his face.

"The force is with us," Haley whispered to him as she passed.

Inside, she stopped a moment to let her eyes adjust to the feeble light filtering in through a dingy window. A strong odor of horse manure assaulted Haley's nose from a wheelbarrow full of dirty hay. It stood by the tack room, waiting to be hauled away. With the horses out in the corral, the stalls looked sad and dreary. The door to the tack room was ajar, but the light was off and Rags was gone.

"Where should we start?" asked Zach, looking around.

Haley scanned the aisle leading to the back of the stable. It was hard-packed earth sprinkled with bits of old hay. At the very end, a ladder led up to a loft filled with hay bales used for fresh bedding for the horses.

"This way," said Haley. She held the apple branch by its forked ends out in front of her and started moving slowly down the aisle. Zach and Vivica followed. They all seemed to be holding their breaths.

After a few steps, Zach peered over her shoulder. "What's happening?" he whispered.

"Nothing yet," replied Haley, her voice also

hushed, as if talking out loud would break some kind of magic spell.

"What's supposed to happen?" asked Vivica.

Haley turned in a slow circle. "When the dowser gets over a place with water, the branch is supposed to jiggle."

They watched the branch. It didn't move.

Haley continued inching her way into the darkness at the end of the horse stalls. She stopped. "I think it moved!"

Vivica stepped in front of Zach. "Let me try," she said, placing her hand on Haley's arm. The branch wiggled.

"Oh!" cried Haley. "Do that again. Hold on to my wrists."

Vivica wrapped her warm hands around Haley's wrists. Haley held tight to the branch ends. They both gasped as it began to shake, first a little twitch and more until the branch bounced up and down like a see-saw.

"You're making it shake," scoffed Zach.

"I am not!" insisted Haley, surprised by the invisible force that was pulling and twisting the apple branch.

"It's doing it all by—" Glancing up, Vivica's voice

caught in a cry. She jumped backward into Zach, pulling Haley with her. They tumbled down in a heap just as huge hay bale flew by them and crashed to the ground. Dust and bits of hay exploded into the air.

All three of them stared at the bale.

"Man, that was close!" breathed Zach.

Haley looked up. Standing at the edge of the loft, a pitchfork in his hands, was Bill Craig.

"What are you kids doing down there?" he yelled. "You coulda been killed with that thing."

"No kidding!" said Vivica, getting up and brushing herself off. "You should watch what you're doing, Gramps. I swear, this place gets more dangerous by the day."

Haley stood and massaged her arm, grateful nothing felt broken.

Bill Craig tossed the pitchfork aside and climbed down the ladder. "Is everyone all right?" he asked when he got down.

Zach flexed his legs. "I guess so. We were looking for an old well."

"Old well?" Mr. Craig scratched his chin, thinking. Then he nodded. "You must mean where the pump is now." He pointed into the corner, a few feet from where they stood. An electric motor hummed by tall water tank resting on a cement foundation. "Your uncle thought this would be handier for the horses and cleaning up," he explained. "Is that what you wanted?"

"We had hoped for treasure," Haley blurted out, then bit her lip, realizing her mistake.

"Really?" said Vivica, eyeing her suspiciously. "I thought you were only interested in finding water."

"We are—we were," said Zach, shooting a warning look toward Haley. "That's what she meant. A treasure of water."

"I was showing them how to dowse for water," explained Haley. "It worked, too."

Mr. Craig snorted. "Of course it worked! You were standing right by the pump."

"It was cool how that stick moved!" said Vivica, ignoring his skepticism. "Mother Nature's power is just awesome!"

"We thought the stables were empty when we started." Haley pointed toward the hayloft. "What were you doing up there, Mr. Craig?"

He hesitated before answering. "I thought I'd give Rags a hand. Used to help your grandpa in the old days. I guess I didn't realize the job had gotten so risky." He turned and started back up the ladder. "You kids run along now so I can finish up."

Haley stared down at the bale of hay. Her dowsing branch now stuck out from underneath it, the way she would have been if Vivica hadn't pulled her aside.

But something else bothered her, too. Why was a seventy-year-old guest shoving heavy hay bales around? Vivica was right. The ranch was getting more dangerous and these "accidents" were adding up.

18

*H*ALEY BURST INTO THE HOUSE, anxious to tell Jake about the accident with the hay bale. She was halfway through the lobby before she spotted him standing by the fireplace hearth. Across from him, Aquanetta sat on the sofa dressed in jeans and sparkly fringed shirt like a real rodeo queen. Her new guitar case rested by her feet and she held a sheaf of papers in her hand.

"Hey there, Haley," said Jake, waving her closer. "Guess what? Miz Real here tells me we have a friend in common—Jimmy. But she tells me he's passed on. She's his widow."

"Oh," said Haley, stopping to catch her breath. "Small world." This was old news to Haley, but she wanted to hear how Aquanetta explained it. "How come you didn't tell us before?"

Aquanetta put the papers down on her lap and smoothed them, taking her time in answering. "I know I should have said something. But being anonymous is nice once in a while. When you're in the public eye, you learn to value times when no one knows who you are."

Haley nodded. That reasoning sounded very familiar. "I know. My mom is the same way. She won't even go to the grocery store because people will recognize her and point at her. One time someone asked her to autograph their box of Cheerios."

Aquanetta raised her eyebrows.

"Haley's mom is a television news anchor," Jake explained.

"I understand," said Aquanetta, nodding. "There's never any time when you can be down or look sloppy. And before an opening night it makes me a nervous wreck." She put her papers aside and walked over to the window and stared outside. The afternoon sunlight bathed the red rocks, making them glow.

"Jimmy told me how beautiful Sedona was, but he forgot to tell me that it was so enchanting." She folded her arms and sighed. "Since coming here, the music has just flowed out of me. I've written five new songs this week."

Jake smiled, making his eyes all crinkly. "That's Red Rock Fever at it's best. Folks come up here and something happens to them. They decide to dump their office jobs in New York and move. They start climbing rocks like mountain goats or chanting to the stars. I'm not surprised that you've got music in your head."

Aquanetta reached into her jeans pocket and drew out a small envelope and handed it to Jake. "I brought a couple of guest passes to the show tomorrow night. I'd be honored if you and Haley would come."

Haley stepped forward to see the tickets. "Thanks!" she said. "That would be great."

Jake nodded. "You bet we'll come. In fact, I'm going to buy up some more tickets and treat all the guests to your show. That is, if it's not sold out already."

"No, not yet. I sure appreciate the support." She gathered up her music papers, grabbed her guitar and started for the front door. "Don't look for me at dinner, Jake. There's a full rehearsal at the park tonight. Someone said they'd give us sandwiches."

After she left, Jake rose from the hearth and stared out the window at the mountains. "She's right, you know. I've been so wrapped up in problems with this place, I've forgotten to enjoy it myself." He turned back to Haley. "Was there something you wanted to see me about?"

Haley sighed. He was in such a good mood, she hated to spoil it by asking questions—questions about the same problems he was trying to ignore. She shifted on her feet. "I came in to ask why Mr. Craig is working in the stables. Zach, Vivica, and I almost got clobbered by a hay bale he tossed down. He said he was helping Rags."

"Hmm. That's not good," said Jake. "I'll have to talk to him about how he can best help out. Bill's been getting antsy lately. Guess retirement isn't as exciting as he and Martha thought it would be."

"Is your computer all fixed?"

"Not yet. Martha's still working on it. But it looks like she'll get all my records back. Amazing!"

"Now are you convinced that someone is trying to hurt your business?"

Jake stared at the floor a moment before answering. "I don't know what to think about that. And as for the business, Bill and Martha Craig have made me an interesting offer."

"An offer? You're not selling the ranch, are you?"

Jake waved his hands defensively. "No, no. It's more like a merger. Martha told me they'd been looking into starting their own bed and breakfast. But after seeing what property costs nowadays, they decided it would be better to buy into an established business instead. They both want to help out, Martha in the office and Bill doing odds and ends. And Rags has been after me to get him some help lately."

Haley considered this news. It made sense with all the real estate information she'd seen in their cabin and what Vivica had told her. Maybe buying into Rockabye Ranch would be a better deal than starting from scratch.

One more question bugged her. Haley took a deep breath.

"Rags has worked for you a long time, hasn't he?"

"Five years this July," said Jake. "Why?"

She hesitated. "Now don't get mad at me for asking this. It's just that with all the trouble you've had lately . . . "

"You think Rags is involved?"

"I heard something about his past, that he'd been in jail."

"Who told you that?'

"Miss Little. At the library."

Jake waved her off. "That's all ancient history. He was a kid, a teenager, just a few years older than you are. He and his buddies thought they'd get some kicks from blowing up mailboxes. They didn't know that was a felony. Plus, the mailbox that Rags blew up—Thelma Little's mailbox—started a grass fire that spread to her garage. She exaggerated a mite when she said he'd been in jail. It was juvenile detention."

"Blowing up things? Starting a fire?" Haley gasped. "And you're not worried about having him around here with all that's happened?"

"Not one bit. He's put all that wildness behind him."

Haley blinked at her uncle. "Am I the only one around here who thinks you—maybe all of us—are in danger?"

Jake shrugged. "Looks that way," he said, heading for his office.

Haley threw up her arms and collapsed on the sofa in disbelief.

19

*F*IFTEEN MINUTES LATER, Haley was still trying to figure out her uncle's attitude when Alma approached her. "This needs filling," she said, holding out an empty snack basket.

Haley groaned, grabbed the basket and lumbered into the pantry. She was in no mood to be fussing with dumb snacks. Why wasn't Jake taking her seriously? Was she overreacting? As she sorted through the packages of candy and chips, she thought about each troubling event of the past few days, starting with the cabin fire. Suddenly, she stopped and stared at the package in her hand. Potato chips. The crinkly kind.

Marty Thomas had said the fire might have been started using crinkly potato chips. Had the firebug just snagged chips from the snack basket? It always sat on the desk with a little honor box for guests to drop in their payment. Since Jake had no vending machines yet, he had thought a basket would be the easiest way to provide snacks. But this discovery hardly narrowed things down. Anyone who came into the lobby would have access to the snack basket, not just the guests.

As Haley returned the snack basket to the front desk, the phone rang. She picked it up and tried to sound professional.

"Rockabye Ranch. How can I help you?"

"Hi, sweetie! How's it going?"

"Mom! I'm so glad you called."

"What's the matter? Are you all right?"

"Yes, I'm fine. I'm just happy to hear your voice."

"I was worried about you. Your father e-mailed me about the fire there. Is everything okay now?"

Haley took the phone and scooted out the front door to the porch where she could talk without anyone listening. Even so, she kept her voice low. "A lot of weird things have been going on. Nothing else major like the fire. But I think someone is trying to ruin Uncle Jake's business."

"Really? What makes you think that?"

"Well, two nights ago the horses were let out of the corral. It took Jake and Rags half the morning to round them all up. Then last night Jake's computer got messed with. All his files were lost."

"Hmm. There could be a logical explanation for all of that."

"Yeah, but there's more." Haley looked around to make double sure no one was near. "Someone has been sending Jake threatening postcards. He thinks it's just a prank, but I don't agree."

"Threats? I don't like the sound of that. What kind of threats?"

Haley twisted a strand of hair, hoping her mom wasn't going to freak out. "They're short notes, kind of vague. One was a picture of some Indian ruins. The message said he should stop or he'd be in ruins. Another one said 'Your time is up.' The latest one has 'Say your prayers' on it and a picture of a church."

"Any signature on those cards?

"No, not really. The last one had initials, S.A.D. Do we know anyone with those initials?"

Mom was quiet so long Haley thought the connection was broken.

"Mom? Are you there?"

"Yes, honey, I'm here."

Haley noticed her voice sounded more worried now.

"S.A.D. isn't a person, it's a group," she explained. "It stands for 'Stop Another Development.' They're loosely organized and very secretive. They tend to target big resorts and housing developments."

"What do they do?"

"They—um—burn them down."

"Oh!" Chills covered Haley's arms and neck. She hadn't thought a whole group might be causing trouble.

"Listen, Haley," continued Mom, "I don't think a group like that would be interested in Jake's place. It's way too small. Plus, S.A.D. doesn't hit places that are inhabited. So far, they've only sabotaged places under construction. They hit and run."

Haley was quiet a moment. She remembered now a story her mom had reported about some unfinished houses getting burned in Tucson. No one was caught, but the police thought S.A.D. was involved.

"Has Jake called the sheriff?" asked Mom.

"No. He won't do it. He's got some problem with his insurance. I think he's hoping this will all go away."

"I don't like the sound of this, Haley. I'm going to call Dad and have him come get you out of there.

This is just the kind of situation I've wanted to keep you out—"

"No, Mom. I want to stay. I've been nosing around, asking questions. I want to know who's doing this. Jake's counting on me to be his extra eyes and ears."

Her mom gave a short laugh. "You sound like a budding investigative reporter."

"I'm just keeping up the family tradition, Mom."

Her mom sighed. "Okay. But promise me one thing. If anything else happens, call the sheriff. No matter what Jake says."

"I promise," said Haley. "How's your job going?"

"It's the same old stupid TV nonsense, only it rains all the time." She paused. "I miss you guys. And the Arizona sunshine."

"I miss you, too, Mom."

At breakfast the next morning Jake made an announcement.

"As you all know," he began, glancing over at Aquanetta, "Miz Real here is going to sing tonight at the Oak Creek Folk Concert."

Mr. and Mrs. Craig burst into gentle applause.

Aquanetta bowed her head toward them and smiled.

Jake continued. "I'm inviting you all to attend as my guests. I'll have Alma fix us up some picnic boxes. This is an outdoor shindig. Everyone sits on the grass, real casual like." He turned to Alma and added, "You and Rags gotta come, too. I'll have him drive you."

Smiling, Alma blushed and answered, "Okay."

Haley liked picturing Rags and Alma on a date. They made a much better couple than Vivica and Rags.

Vivica raised her hand. "Um, what time does all this start?"

Jake looked over at Aquanetta for help.

"I have to be there early, of course," she explained, "but I'm told the public can show up anytime to have their dinners. The concert itself starts at seven."

"I can take us all in the hotel van," added Jake. "We'll meet here on the porch, say, about five. How's that sound to everyone?"

Again, Vivica raised her hand. "Thanks, but I'll drive myself. I'm hiking up the canyon this afternoon and I may not be back by the time you all leave."

"Well, all right then," said Jake. "I'll leave your ticket at the box office and you can pick it up when you get there."

Mr. Craig rubbed his palms together. "Sounds like a plan." He and Mrs. Craig got up and followed Aquanetta toward the pool, chatting excitedly with her about the upcoming concert.

"This will be so much more fun than watching old movies," gushed Mrs. Craig.

Zach jumped up and bounded down the porch steps. Haley wanted to talk to him, but Alma handed her a tray and nodded toward the tables and the dirty dishes waiting to be cleared.

At five o'clock, Jake, Haley and the Craigs gathered on the porch, ready to leave. Alma brought out a cardboard box full of dinner sacks.

Haley noticed Zach wasn't with the group. In fact, she hadn't seen him all day. She went looking for him and found him up by the corral, watching the horses.

"Where have you been?" she asked. She noticed he had his old map in his hands.

"Exploring. No luck, though," Zach answered.

"Everyone's about to leave for the concert. You coming?"

"Nope. Tell your uncle thanks and all, but I'll stay here."

"Why?"

"Mom didn't want to say anything this morning, but she really doesn't like me being at her openings. It's some kind of superstition she has. She's afraid I'll see her goof up or something."

Haley glanced at her watch. Vivica had been gone all afternoon, too, and still wasn't back. "Then I'll stay here, too. Let me go tell Jake we're waiting for Vivica. That way you don't have to explain anything to him about your mom's superstitions."

Zach smiled. "Thanks. I knew you'd understand."

Haley grinned back at him then jogged back to the house to tell Jake their plans. A few minutes later, standing in the drive, Haley waved good-bye as Jake's van and Rags's pickup drove off down Boynton Pass Road.

20

BY A QUARTER TO SIX, Vivica still wasn't back. The ranch was quiet. Haley and Zach sat on the floor of the lobby eating their sack dinners and playing Scrabble.

Haley couldn't concentrate. With each minute, she grew more worried. Where was Vivica? Was she lost? Why hadn't she come back yet? Other thoughts made her uneasy, too. She kept thinking about her phone call with Mom and how the members of S.A.D. liked to strike places that were uninhabited, or deserted like the ranch was now. The fact that she and Zach were still there was a last-minute change, if anyone had been watching for an opportunity.

Haley shoved her tiles aside. "I'm going to run over to Vivica's cabin and see if she's back."

Zach studied his rack of letter tiles. "Fine. That'll give me time to figure out a word using E, O, I, I, and J."

At the cabin door, Haley paused, then knocked.

"Vivica?"

No answer.

She tried the door. It was locked. Haley fished out her ring of cabin keys and opened the door. After all, she could be there on maid business.

"Housekeeping!" she called into the room.

The bed was unmade and towels lay scattered everywhere. But all of Vivica's belongings were packed up. Her backpack and duffle bag sat by the door. A familiar sweet scent also hung in the air. Haley checked the ashtray. It was full of small stubs of incense nestled in a pile of gray ash. She bent closer and sniffed. In a flash, she remembered where else she'd smelled something like this.

That night, in Jake's office, the person who knocked her over had this scent on her. Haley squeezed her eyes shut, remembering the scene. As she did so, another image grew. One of incense burning slowly, slowly. Hadn't Marty Thomas suggested the fire began with some kind of delay device? He was thinking of a cigarette. But a chunk of incense would work, too, thought Haley. And Haley remembered that first morning when she cleaned Vivica's cabin, empty snack bags had littered the table.

She closed the cabin door and ran back to the house. A feeling of dread sat in her stomach like a stone. Was her imagination running wild? Was she jumping to conclusions? If only she could be sure.

Zach met her on the porch steps. "Vivica just phoned."

"She did? Where is she?"

He pointed up toward the red cliffs. "She's stuck in that cave. Says she's twisted her ankle and can't walk. We need to go help her down."

Haley narrowed her eyes. "If she's in that cave, how could she phone?"

"She had her cell phone with her."

"Yeah, I bet." Haley bit her lip, trying to sort out what she should do. If Vivica really was hurt, Jake would expect them to go help her. But what if her suspicions were right? Were they falling into a trap? She was not eager to climb up to that cave to find out.

Zach stood halfway out the door, looking impatient. "So, let's go!"

"Wait a sec," Haley said, running down the hall to her room. "I have to get something first."

Moments later, the two were hiking up the hill behind the ranch, passing the "vortex" circle Vivica had laid out. Beyond that point, the ground turned steep and rocky. Haley lost her footing several times on the crumbly parts, and Zach had to catch her to stop her from tumbling down the slope. Just before they reached the cave, the path gave out completely. Zach stopped and stared up at the sheer rock wall. Below them, the ground fell away into an arroyo.

"Now what?" he asked.

Haley pointed to a small opening near the base of the wall. It was about the size of a child's wagon. "See that crack? We crawl through that."

Down on their bellies, they wiggled through like a couple of lizards to the other side. There, the path snaked upward again, hugging the red cliff. Haley kept her eyes on the trail, trying not to look to her left, into the rocky gully below. After about thirty yards, the path widened to form a shelf at the base of the cave. The old wooden ladder still leaned against the face of the cliff, leading up to the cave. It looked even worse than Haley had remembered. The first rung was missing and some of the others looked cracked.

Haley cupped her hands to her mouth. "Vivica! Are you there?" Her words echoed off the canyon walls.

A voice called out from above, "Up here!"

"If we steady the ladder, can you climb down?" Haley asked.

"No. I think my ankle's broken," yelled Vivica. "You have to come up."

Zach looked at the ladder and shrugged. "If she got up there with this, I guess we can, too." He started up the first step. "Let's go get her."

Haley stared at the rickety ladder, then up at the cave. A wave of fear washed over her. "No way. You go. I'll wait here. I'm scared of heights, and wobbly old ladders don't help. You can get her down from up there, can't you?"

"I'll try." Zach stretched his foot to the first good rung and pulled himself up. Slowly he rose, one step at a time, testing the rungs as he climbed. Haley steadied the ladder at the bottom. When he reached the top, he hesitated, then climbed into the cave. Haley could hear him talking to Vivica. After a few moments, his face appeared above her.

"She needs both of us for this to work. Come on. I'll help you at the top. That's the hardest part."

Haley froze. One part of her wanted to leave Vivica in the cave. It would serve her right for causing so much trouble. But what if she was hurt?

What if all Haley's suspicions were wrong? She glanced down behind her. If she fell, she might crash onto the hard shelf or plunge into the arroyo below. There wasn't much room for error.

"Hurry!" Zach urged. He jabbed his finger toward the horizon. "It'll be dark soon, and then it will be harder."

Haley took a deep breath. She had to try. One foot, one hand at a time, she started up. She pressed her body close to the old ladder, creeping slowly up. Her hands trembled as she reached for each rung. Her feet tested them just as Zach had done. So far, so good. Then halfway up, the rotten wood under her foot splintered. Her foot slipped down, scraping on the splintery edge of the ladder. She gripped the rung above tighter, her knuckles white. Tears welled in her eyes as she willed her body to stop shaking. Haley blinked away her tears and looked up.

"You can do it!" Zach said. "Put your foot on the broken end of the rung then quickly pull yourself up. Just don't look down."

She had no choice. Going down was just as scary as going up. She gently stepped on the broken rung and moved up. Hand over hand, foot after foot, she kept climbing.

Finally, Zach's arms reached down and grabbed hers, hoisting her up over the edge and into the floor of the cave.

"Cave" was probably the wrong word. Eons of wind and water had carved out a huge room like a band shell from the sandstone. The dirt and rock floor stretched about thirty feet across and about twenty feet deep. Soot from years of cook fires had left black streaks across the ceiling, which slanted downward until it met with the floor and merged with smaller cracks toward the back. Vivica sat in the darkness, near a wall of stacked rocks, her ankle wrapped in a T-shirt. Next to her was a coil of rope and a pair of binoculars.

"How'd you hurt your ankle?" Haley asked.

"Stumbled on a rock after I got up here," Vivica answered, pointing to a pile of flat sandstone rocks that had once formed part of a protective wall at the edge of the cave.

"So, what's the plan?" said Zach, eyeing the rope.

Vivica picked it up and began making a loop. "I'm going to tie this around my waist. Then one of you can guide me down the ladder while the other holds on to the rope from up here—in case I slip." She paused. "Hey, you know that treasure you two have been so hot to find? Well, there's a bundle stuck into some rocks back there." She jerked her thumb at a dark cleft in the wall. "Could be what you've been looking for."

Zach grinned at Haley. "Told you! Told you this was where he'd hide it!"

They scurried into the shadows, scanning the ground and crevices. Old corncobs, bits of charred wood, and pottery shards littered the floor. Great treasures if they'd been looking for signs of ancient cultures. But no bundle.

"Where did you see—?" Haley turned back toward Vivica, but she wasn't there. The rope wasn't coiled on the ground, either. It was sliding free over the edge of the cave.

21

ZACH AND HALEY RUSHED to the edge, expecting to see Vivica splattered on the ground below. Instead, she stood there staring up at them, rewinding the rope in big loops. There was obviously nothing at all wrong with her ankle.

"You won't be needing this, either," she said, giving the ladder a shove. It crashed down, breaking into a cloud of dust and splintered wood.

"Why'd you do that? Now we're stuck," Haley wailed.

"Not my problem. You guys were supposed to go with the others." She tapped her binoculars. "When I saw that you didn't leave, I had to get you out of there. You're much better off up in that cave than down at the ranch." Vivica glanced at her watch. "Soon the fires will start. With everyone gone now, no one gets hurt."

"But why are you doing this?" asked Haley.

"Protest," said Vivica. "People like your uncle can't go on scraping the land, building hotels and golf courses, and destroying all of nature's beauty. And after I found that new vortex site, I was even more sure I had to protect the area."

"The computer? The fences? That was all your doing, too?" asked Haley, her anger rising. "Are you with S.A.D.?"

Vivica shrugged. "Not exactly. I knew about S.A.D. and the fires set in Phoenix and Tucson. Protest by fire. I liked that. No one got hurt, but it made a strong statement."

"But why pick on Jake?" asked Haley. "Rockabye Ranch is not some big resort."

"This was easier to get at. When the Cs showed me the article about your uncle getting weird postcards, I thought I'd send him some warning ones. The TV news has been full of reports about S.A.D. He should have known what it meant."

Not Jake, thought Haley. Not an old cowboy with no TV. "What about your grandparents? Are they in this, too?"

Vivica waved the question away. "No way. They gripe a lot about development, but they were even thinking of copying Jake and starting a hotel, too.

Now maybe they won't." She looped the rope over her shoulder and headed down the trail.

"You won't get away!" Zach shouted after her. "We'll tell the sheriff, and he'll come arrest you."

When she reached the hole in the rock wall, Vivica turned and held up her fist. "He'll have to find me first!"

Haley's panic grew as she watched Vivica slither through the hole and disappear to the other side. Looking over the treetops, she focused on the ranch grounds to see if anything was happening yet. Had Vivica rigged another delayed fire like she had before? So far, no smoke plume rose in the air, but Haley had a feeling it would soon.

She reached in her pocket and pulled out the cell phone she'd brought from her room. "This phone better work. Vivica's did from up here." Haley punched the buttons, saying "Yes!" when the tone came on. She called the sheriff and explained their trouble.

"Are they coming?" asked Zach when she hung up.

"Yeah. I only hope they can get here before it's too late."

"Good. We can sit tight and wait," said Zach,

folding his arms.

"No, we can't," said Haley. "What if they don't get there in time? We have to get out of here." She peered over the edge of the cave. "But how?"

Zach scanned the walls of the cave. The back offered no opening. He moved to the far left side and stared downward into a long shadowy crack. "Hey, look at this!" he cried.

Haley moved over to him but stayed back from the edge.

Zach knelt on the cave floor and pointed down the rock walls. "See those small holes? They've been carved into the face of the rock all the way down, in a pattern. I think they're foot- and handholds. I read about how the Sinaguas used handholes like this hundreds of years ago."

Haley crouched on her knees and crept closer. Her stomach lurched when she looked down the crack, trying to follow where Zach was pointing. Two red sandstone slabs had split, forming a cleft like two pieces of bread. Fist-sized indentations led down in a zigzag pattern, just big enough for a hand or foot. Several small rock ledges also jutted out along the way.

The thought of climbing down by her fingers

and toes had Haley's head spinning. She glanced toward the west, where the sun was sinking fast. It took her less than two seconds to realize this was their only hope.

"We have to try," she said. "Once the sun goes down, it'll be too dark. Plus, it'll be too late to stop that firebug."

"Or we could stay put and let the sheriff take care of her," suggested Zach.

Haley gulped. "No. I have to go. If you don't want to try this, I'll send someone back to get you. But I have to go."

Zach shook his head. "You amaze me. Ten minutes ago you were scared to climb a ladder."

"Ten minutes ago I didn't know what Vivica was up to. Are you coming or not?"

He looked down the cleft once again. "Okay. After you. Go slow and make yourself one with the rocks."

"One with the rocks. Sweet. You sound just like Vivica."

"Just take it easy, don't hurry." He pointed downward. "Once you're on that first ledge you'll be okay."

No, I won't, Haley replied silently. But she had to

try. She had to stop Vivica, and every minute she stalled was a minute lost. Haley tried to swallow, but her throat was dry with fear.

"My feet will fit better in those little holes without shoes," she said, pulling off her clunky canvas shoes and tossing them down to the ground. With one last glance at the cave, Haley grabbed onto a wedge of sandstone, spread her body flat, and swung her feet over the side. After a few seconds of searching for a foothold, she cried out, "Found the ledge. Now for the handholds." She reached across the cleft and placed her hand in a small hole. Then she eased her foot down and placed it in a hole on the opposite wall. Crablike, she straddled the cleft, inching her way down, from one tiny hole to another.

About halfway down, her foot slipped sending dust and bits of rock raining down to the ledge below. She froze for a moment, her fingers clinging to gritty little handholds, one foot wedged into a hole while the other tapped madly for the next one.

"I can't do this!" she cried.

"Yes, you can," said Zach, his voice calm. "Don't panic. There's a foothold just a little farther down on your left."

She found it. Zach's voice guided her down until

she jumped to level ground. Brushing the dirt from her hands, she called up to him, "I did it! Now you come. I'll be your guide."

Zach yanked off his shoes, too, and tossed them down before descending. As soon as he joined her on the ground, they pulled on their shoes and scrambled through the crawl hole. Twilight shadows stretched across the canyon, making the trail hard to follow. Haley kept her eyes fixed on the ground as she scrabbled down the slope, hoping there was still time to stop Vivica.

22

As they neared the ranch, they were startled to see Blaze and Misty galloping toward them in the dusky light. The horses whinnied, their eyes wild, then veered off into the brush.

"She's let the horses loose again," cried Haley, pointing to three other horses nervously prancing along the arroyo.

The lights from the ranch house and cabins came into view, and Haley was relieved to see the buildings were still okay. The barbecue deck, however, made her suck in her breath. Vivica had piled the wooden chairs and tables in the center and was circling around it, shaking a can as she went. A soft breeze brought the smell of pungent fumes.

Zach jerked to a stop. "Gasoline!"

"Let's get her, before she lights it all," said Haley, taking off again.

Zach raced ahead of her, past the stables and corral, zeroing in behind Vivica. He lunged at her, grabbing the can. Gasoline sloshed onto his shirt as Vivica spun around, tugging the can away from him.

Her free hand slipped into her pocket and pulled out a small lighter. "Back off!" she snapped, holding the lighter toward him.

Zach let go and stepped slowly away, his hands up in surrender.

"Take it easy!" said Haley, trying to keep her voice calm. "If you start a fire, it'll spread to the whole place."

Vivica placed her thumb on the lighter, her eyes glistening intensely. "Then don't interfere. You two should have stayed put. I really don't want to hurt anyone. The timing was perfect tonight, with everyone gone to the concert."

Zach took a step toward her. "Why did you burn our cabin?"

"It was supposed to be vacant," Vivica said. "I didn't know you'd switched cabins."

"But why?" asked Haley. "What did Jake ever do to you?"

"I told you. It's not about him. It's about the environment. "

"A fire won't help the environment or the horses," argued Haley.

"The horses are free to run now. They won't be hurt," countered Vivica. She turned the gas can over and dribbled a line of gasoline toward the gnarly old sycamore tree at the end of the deck. When the can was empty, she tossed it aside. "Time to give this so-called dude ranch back to nature." She clicked the lighter and a yellow flame danced on the tip. With a flick of her wrist she tossed the lighter in the dirt.

Haley gasped as a trail of fire shot across the ground like an angry snake. It sped up the sycamore tree, igniting the dry leaves and branches. In seconds, the tree became a blazing torch and a dark column of smoke soared into the darkening sky. Ash and cinders rained down on the jumble of chairs and tables.

"I'll get a hose," yelled Zach, running toward the house.

Vivica grabbed Haley's arm, pulling her away from the heat of the flames. "Give it up!"

Haley squirmed away from her grasp. "No!"

In moments, the pile of chairs on the deck turned it into a bonfire that crackled and collapsed, sending up more sparks. Bits of charred wood skittered across the ground, leaving a trail of hot cinders.

Sirens wailed in the distance and panic washed over Vivica's face.

"You're on your own, then," Vivica yelled as she grabbed her backpack and bolted for her van. She backed up and tore down the drive, passing a Sheriff's Department truck with blinking lights headed for the house. Haley held her breath, willing the truck to block Vivica's escape. But her hopes faded as the van careened around the truck and disappeared down Boynton Pass Road. Haley ran to the parking area as two officers climbed out of their truck.

"Why didn't you stop her?" she demanded, pointing at the van's trail of dust.

"This looks a more important," said one officer, darting past her. "The fire department is on the way. Is there a water pump here?"

Haley pointed toward the pool. "Yes. Over there."

The two men hustled over to the pool. Zach directed them to the pump Jake had installed, and in minutes they had a steady stream of water aimed at the fire. For the second time in a week, clouds of acrid steam rose into the air.

Haley darted into the laundry room and came back with two plastic buckets. She and Zach teamed up, scooping water from the pool and flinging it on the fire until the fire crew arrived and took over.

Exhausted and dirty, Haley retreated to a step on the porch.

Zach trotted over and slumped down beside her. "Help got here fast. Good thing you brought your cell phone along when we left."

"I had a bad feeling about Vivica's call," Haley answered. "When she claimed she was hurt up in the cave, I thought she might need a rescue crew. But a little voice inside me warned that it might also be a trap."

Haley sighed, her shoulders sagging. "Now I wish we'd left her up there. She got away."

"But we stopped her from burning the whole place down. Just think if we hadn't been here."

Haley turned to him. "Yeah. Your mom was right to be nervous about opening night. Only the trouble was here, not at the concert."

When the fire finally sputtered out, the officers went back to the truck to put out an alert for Vivica.

Zach and Haley stood by the ashes of the deck. Only the stone barbecue and chimney had survived intact, coated with streaks of black soot. The old sycamore tree that had once shaded Caleb Marshall's cabin was now a blackened claw.

Feeling sorry for the old tree, Haley scooped one more bucket of water from the pool and hurled it at the charred trunk, hoping to stop any more destruction. The tree seemed to sigh in relief as steam hissed from hot spots. The fire had consumed all the branches and collections of dried leaves, laying bare a twisted main trunk and exposing a deep, hollow core.

As Haley peered into the dark hole, her heart started to race. She blinked, hoping her eyes weren't playing tricks on her. There, nestled at the center and black with age and grime, sat an old metal box. Slowly, it dawned on her that she had found Caleb's Cache.

23

*I*T WAS WAY PAST MIDNIGHT, but all the lights blazed in the ranch house. Jake and the others were still recovering from the shock of coming home to another fire after the concert. The sheriff questioned everyone, and then everyone questioned Haley and Zach. Aquanetta, still dressed in her spangled concert outfit, couldn't stop hugging them, saying they were heroes.

After tears and embarrassed apologies to Jake, Martha and Bill Craig left with the sheriff to answer questions about Vivica and where she might be headed.

Everyone else gathered in the lobby, waiting for Rags and Jake to bring in the old metal box Haley had found. The room smelled like apple pie as Alma passed around mugs of hot apple cider.

Jake and Rags bustled in the door and plunked

the old iron box on the coffee table. Everyone hushed as they came close to stare at it.

"That baby sure was wedged in tight," said Jake. "Like the tree had grown around it, sealing it in there."

"It took some doing, but I got the dang lock off," said Rags, holding up a hacksaw. "Now let's see what we got here." He pushed up the lid with his thumbs and turned the box over.

A leather coin pouch thudded onto the table, along with some folded papers and a bundle of old letters. Right away, Zach grabbed the pouch, opened the clasp, and dumped out twenty silver dollars. Disappointment filled his eyes.

"That's it? Twenty bucks? That's the treasure?" he cried.

Jake sorted through the coins and picked one up. "Could be worth more. These are from 1922. Let me see if I can find something about this on the Internet."

While Jake went into his office to look up coin values, Haley unfolded one of the old yellowed papers.

"What is this?" she asked, holding it out to Rags.

A fancy design of eagles and curlicue ribbons framed the wording, TWO HUNDRED SHARES— Arizona Minerals Exchange Company.

"Looks like an old stock certificate from the mines up in Jerome." He glanced through the other certificates and shook his head. "I doubt they're worth anything. Those mining companies folded years ago."

Haley frowned and shoved the papers aside. "Too bad. I thought we were rich."

Her eyes fell to the bundle of letters. She untied the string around them and slid one out. The old envelope had a simple address: Caleb Marshall, General Delivery, Sedona, Arizona. Gently pulling out the folded letter inside, she read a few lines and smiled.

"Oooh! These are love letters! Maybe Mr. Marshall wasn't such a hermit after all."

Aquanetta picked up the bundle. "They were obviously a treasure to Mr. Marshall. He didn't want anyone else reading them. At least not while he was alive." She sat down on the sofa, opened another letter and started reading silently.

Jake came back from the office, a slight smile on his face. "Caleb had the right idea about saving silver dollars. Too bad he picked the wrong year. Plus, the coins aren't brand new."

Zach held up his hands. "So, what are they worth?"

"About ten dollars each, I think," Jake said.

Haley poked Jake in the side. "Fifty-fifty split, like you promised Zach's dad?"

Jake rubbed his chin, thinking. "Let's see. You two saved Rockabye Ranch and all my investment from a loco arsonist. Yeah, that's worth about a hundred bucks each!"

Zach sighed.

Jake patted his back, grinning. "Just kidding! You guys saved my bacon tonight, and I got no idea how to thank you."

It was late and had been a busy day and night so everyone started saying their good-nights. On the way out, Aquanetta paused by Jake, the bundle of letters in her hand.

"May I borrow these? I'd like to read through them."

Jake shrugged. "Sure. Keep 'em if you like. They're not worth anything to me."

Aquanetta held the bundle to her chest and smiled. "Don't be too sure about that."

The next morning was check-out day. Haley stretched out on one of the porch chairs waiting for everyone to leave. She had one more round of cabin cleaning with Alma before the new guests arrived. But for now, she leaned her head back and let the sun warm her.

Too many thoughts tumbled her brain. She needed to focus. She stared up at the mountains, noticing again how the rocks changed with the light, taking on new personalities, like clouds do. A rock shape that looked like a boat one minute, morphed into a crouching lion the next. Changing, like people do.

Haley recognized some of the changes going on in her, too. Helping to save Jake's ranch had made her feel more confident, more independent. She thought back on the phone call with her Mom. There had definitely been a touch of pride in Mom's voice when she'd called her a "budding investigative reporter." Was Mom finally realizing that she could handle herself in the Big Bad World? Maybe I should cut her some slack, thought Haley. Maybe we're both learning to let go.

"Working hard or hardly working?" a familiar voice asked her.

She sat up with a start. "Dad! You're back!"

He looked toward the ruined deck and its pile of charred furniture. "What happened?"

"Wait till you hear!"

As Haley walked with him into the house, she filled him in on Vivica's misguided plan to burn the ranch. When he'd heard the whole story, he shook his head.

"I only wanted you to get some work experience," he said. "I had no idea it would turn so dangerous. You should have called me."

"But I'm okay, Dad," insisted Haley. "I 'rose to the occasion' as you and Mom are always telling me to do."

He gave her a hug. "That you did! And now are you ready to come home to boring old Tucson?"

Haley pulled out of his embrace. "Actually, Dad, I'd like to stay on a couple more weeks. Jake still needs me here."

He placed his hands on her shoulders, giving her an appraising look. "You do, huh? Well, only for two weeks. After that, we're flying up to Seattle. Your mother has found a newspaper job I might like.

And, she's promised to take us on some ferryboat rides. What do you think?"

Haley felt her whole body relax. "Does this mean we're going to be a whole family again?"

"You bet, kiddo. You bet!"

Jake met them in the lobby, giving them both bear hugs. "This young lady was great," he said. "Especially when she refused to keep her nose outta my troubles. I just got off the phone with the sheriff. Vivica and her boyfriend were picked up in Nogales buying train tickets to Mexico."

"What will happen to her?" asked Haley.

Jake shook his head. "Don't know yet. She's gotten herself into serious trouble this time. I hope she gets counseling, not jail."

"She really didn't want to hurt anyone," said Haley.

Jake nodded. "Rockabye Ranch may have gotten off to a shaky start, but things will run smoother now that I've got partners."

Haley's dad arched his eyebrows. "Partners?"

"Yup. Bill and Martha Craig have bought into the place and are going to stay on to help me run it," explained Jake. "They feel partly responsible for what Vivica did. I tried to reassure them it wasn't their fault, but they still feel awful about it anyway."

Aquanetta appeared in the doorway with Zach behind her carrying a suitcase and the new guitar. "Time to check out," she said, handing Haley her cabin key.

Haley cocked her head. "Heading back to Houston?"

Aquanetta put her arm around Zach and smiled. "No. We're going to look for an apartment in town."

"You're staying in Sedona?" asked Jake.

"I just got off the phone with the manager of the Enchantment Resort," said Aquanetta. "He was at the concert last night and liked my music. He's offered me a job!"

"That's swell!" said Jake. He looked over at Zach. "If you're going to be nearby, Rags could sure use some help from time to time with the horses. Interested?"

Zach's face lit up. "Yeah!"

Aquanetta reached into her big tote bag and drew out the bundle of letters. "I sat up last night reading these. They really are a treasure, you know, a tale of lost love and tragedy. It was a broken heart that turned Mr. Marshall into a hermit."

"Humpf," muttered Jake. "Who'd have thought that of the old guy?"

"Last night you said these letters weren't worth anything to you," reminded Aquanetta. "But what if I write a song called 'The Ballad of Rockabye Ranch'? That love story could make this place famous!"

Jake grinned at her.

"Maybe even infamous," added Haley.